THE GARDEN GOD

VALANCOURT CLASSICS

THE GARDEN GOD

A Tale of Two Boys

BY

FORREST REID

'Take this kiss upon the brow!'

EDGAR ALLAN POE

'Yea, to Love himself is pour'd
  This frail song of hope and fear.
Thou art Love, of one accord
  With kind Sleep to bring him near,
  Still-eyed, deep-eyed, ah, how dear!
  Master, Lord,
In his name implor'd, O hear!'

D. G. ROSSETTI

Edited with an introduction and notes by
Michael Matthew Kaylor

Kansas City:

VALANCOURT BOOKS

2007

The Garden God by Forrest Reid
First published in 1905
First Valancourt Books edition, November 2007

The Garden God and "Pan's Pupil" © 1905 by Forrest Reid
Introduction and notes © 2007 by Michael Matthew Kaylor
This edition © 2007 by Valancourt Books

Library of Congress Cataloguing-in-Publication Data

Reid, Forrest, 1875-1947.
  The garden god : a tale of two boys / by Forrest Reid ; edited with an introduction and notes by Michael Matthew Kaylor. — 1st Valancourt Books ed.
      p. cm. — (Valancourt Classics)
  Includes bibliographical references.
  ISBN 1-934555-04-5
  1. Teenage boys—England—Fiction. 2. Schoolboys—England—Fiction 3. Platonic love—Fiction. 4. Psychological fiction. I. Kaylor, Michael Matthew. II. Title.
  PR6035.E43G28 2007
  823'.912—dc22

                                    2007019550

Composition by James D. Jenkins
Published by Valancourt Books
Kansas City, Missouri
http://www.valancourtbooks.com

CONTENTS

FOREWORD

If a single product only of Hellenic art were to be saved in the wreck of all beside, one might choose perhaps from the "beautiful multitude" of the Panathenaic frieze, that line of youths on horseback, with their level glances, their proud, patient lips, their chastened reins, their whole bodies in exquisite service.

—Walter Pater, from "Winckelmann"

PROVERBIAL questions are often perennial, and among those that people love to loft are the ones that are the most problematic to answer honestly, often beginning with "Imagine that there is a fire, and you can save only one—" or "Imagine that you are on a desert island, and you can have only one—" Avid minds such as Walter Pater have ever puzzled those scenarios of cultural apocalypse.

However, those questions, at least for Western culture, already have foregone answers—Homer's *Iliad*, Leonardo's *Mona Lisa*, Shakespeare's plays, the Gutenberg Bible, Beethoven's *Ninth Symphony*, etc., and etc. We all know the approved answers because every culture is a rather Platonic canon of "The Best," a hierarchy that education is meant to inculcate and cultivate, as any decent education should. In fact, we literally surround ourselves with this hierarchy, as reference points, as propagandistic statements, as projections of our inner lives. This is evident in Forrest Reid's description of his own decorative decisions at 9 South Parade, Belfast:

> The wallpaper is pale green. Many books round the walls [. . .] The pictures I have up are the *Ganymede*, the *Blue Boy* and the *Greek Boy*, which you know already. I have also a beautiful Perugino youth, and an anonymous portrait of a young man—the thing in the Salon Carré. The two boy photographs—you know, the boys sitting on beds that Turner took, are just above the chimney piece: Socrates is over the door and a Whistler is in a corner.

In a similar fashion, I too have my own catalogue, my own hierarchy of "The Best"—Praxiteles' *Hermes*, Caravaggio's *Bacchus*, Bronzino's *Lodovico Capponi*, Hopkins's *Poems*, James's last three novels, Keats's *Letters*, the sole "coloured copy" of Blake's *Jerusa-*

lem, Britten's *War Requiem*—and I too surround myself with these objects in one form or another. Such objects, personalised to taste and environment and background, are how we, as academics and connoisseurs of culture, define and fashion our "selves," construct our worlds, and decorate our "rooms of one's own."

However, for me, such a catalogue of "The Best" is moot. Given those proverbial scenarios of cultural demise, I would certainly respond by instinct rather than hierarchy, by something far more primal, far more personal. As a result, a Heraclitean fire would purge away all of Keats, Hopkins, James, and Britten; the sea would swallow Praxiteles, Caravaggio, Bronzino, and Blake. My entire aesthetic pantheon would either be burned or drowned, for I would be found clutching instead *Tom Barber* (1955), that single volume containing Forrest Reid's "great trilogy of boyhood"—the novels *Young Tom*, *The Retreat*, and *Uncle Stephen*.

"Hyperbole!" is likely what you, my dear reader, are presently thinking. "Tragedy! Insanity!" would likely be the general chorus were I to appear with my bound treasure, save for the puzzled few who would question instead, "*Tom Barber?*"

The figures of Praxiteles, Caravaggio, and Bronzino arrest the gaze, make it linger; Hopkins's "Windhover" is sound made flesh; James's Maggie is the ultimate triumph of character; Keats's thoughts on "Friendship" outrival others' thoughts on "Love"; Britten's music is hauntingly palpable . . . however, Tom Barber is . . . well . . . I am not sure I can . . . see it's because . . .

"Ah, we know that blush" would be the consensus of humanity in response to my stumbling explanation, understanding that "first love" exerts the strongest, the most inexplicable of bonds and obligations and vagaries.

Curiously, prior to this invitation to edit *The Garden God*, I have never so much as mentioned Forrest Reid in print, in the classroom, rarely even in private. Reid has ever been my "secret playmate," a playmate whose texts—nearly sacred, at least to me—have always been read for pleasure, without a clutched pencil, without obligations to anyone save myself and that friend whom some have chosen to dub "The Pan of Ulster." *Forrest Reid*—his very name suggests woodlands and a whittled pipe upon which to play a tune to accompany the refrain of a poem by William Butler Yeats that Reid considered among "The Best," as he explains:

> There is a suggestion of the Pre-Raphaelite school in its minute detail, and it has an adorable freshness and *naïveté*, a kind of happy innocence, a kind of delicate bloom upon it, that is characteristic of many of the early pieces. One of these, indeed, *The Stolen Child*, is to my mind as beautiful a lyric as he ever wrote, as beautiful as any to be found even in the golden age of English poetry [—with its refrain:]

> *Come away, human child!*
> *To the waters and the wild*
> *With a faery, hand in hand,*
> *For the world's more full of weeping than you can understand.*

Reid is, likewise, always invitational, for his is the voice of Pan in this exchange from "Pan's Pupil":

> "Did you not call me to you? Do not be afraid. I will not harm you. You are a human boy, and must live out your destiny. I will not keep you. Someday, however, when the world seems very hard and cold, you will perhaps seek again the door to my fairyland, and if you find it then and enter, it will be to stay for ever and ever." [. . .]

> [And the boy] saw the first beauty of the earth, of silver streams, and golden woods, and violet valleys, and tree-shaded water springs. He saw, in forest glades, fauns and nymphs dancing under the red harvest-moon, and beside haunted pools in whose still water the over-world was mirrored. And he knew that from all these things he had drawn the strength of his life, and he dropped upon his knees and cried: "O Pan, I am your child for evermore, and none save Death shall take me from you."

I have ever been that pupil, whistling that tune sung by "The Pan of Ulster," for "since my childhood I have loved none better [. . .] In my heaven he walks eternally with Shakespeare and the Greeks."

In *Shakespearean Negotiations*, Stephen Greenblatt explains a common, educated "desire to speak with the dead," a desire that he describes as "a familiar, if unvoiced, motive in literary studies, a motive organized, professionalized, buried beneath thick layers of bureaucratic decorum." Perhaps surprisingly, I have never had such a desire in relation to Forrest Reid, for Pan has never really died, a truth that Reid's friend Walter de la Mare ponders:

> They told me Pan was dead, but I
>> Oft marvelled who it was that sang
> Down the green valleys languidly
>> Where the grey elder-thickets hang.

Like that Arcadian god, Forrest Reid lives on—no more so than in his trilogy *Tom Barber*—a place where "the waters and the wild" provide escape when "the world's more full of weeping than you can understand."

The Garden God, one of Reid's earliest works, also provides a "door to fairyland," beyond which the materialism and cares of modern life hold little sway, replaced in their importance by the rarest of restorative qualities—"happiness for happiness' sake." However, this is not a fleeting quality, for there is a blessed constancy to the piped songs of "The Pan of Ulster":

> Ah, happy, happy boughs! that cannot shed
>> Your leaves, nor ever bid the Spring adieu;
> And, happy melodist, unwearied,
>> For ever piping songs for ever new;
> More happy love! more happy, happy love!
>> For ever warm and still to be enjoy'd,
>> For ever panting, and for ever young [. . .]

Reid explains this Keatsian quality to his friend George Buchanan:

> To me the value of a book depends on its charm and that does not lie in the choice of subject but in the spirit that the writer breathes into it. [. . .] The qualities that give a novel long life are poetry and humour—*Wuthering Heights* and *Huckleberry Finn*. These are the books one turns to [. . .]

Among such books is *The Garden God*, one of the first of those piped songs that beckons towards my treasured *Tom Barber*, whose protagonist is truly as Reid describes him:

Tom grew to be extraordinarily real to me—real, I think, in a way none of my other characters has ever been, so that sometimes for a few minutes I would stop writing because he seemed to be actually there in the room. I knew the tones of his voice, I caught glimpses of him in the street, and one evening, after finishing a chapter, I put down my work to go out for a walk with him.

It is on just such a walk that Graham Iddesleigh—the palpable boy whose tale is *The Garden God*, a boy who has been my long-time friend—invites you, his Puckish hands extended. "Give me your hands, if we be friends."

MICHAEL MATTHEW KAYLOR

For Petr Vyhnálek,
who needs no explanation why

INTRODUCTION

The Garden God: A "Setting"

> A fountain coloured by the rainbow of romance, and
> brushed by the outstretched wings of Love.
> — The Garden God[1]

FOR as short a novel as Forrest Reid's *The Garden God: A Tale of Two Boys*, an introduction is perhaps best handled as if attempting to set a delicate cameo into filigree rather than attempting to elucidate—in other words, establishing its context and accentuating its unique beauty rather than providing a detailed interpretation or even a reading strategy. However, opting to approach this novel in this way is not, in the least, a disingenuous attempt to skirt Peter Coveney's claim that "to apply anything like an intelligent criticism to Forrest Reid is to deny his work any justification as responsible literature,"[2] for Reid's work does indeed warrant "intelligent criticism," though it has rarely garnered such attention, for reasons beyond the work itself, as what follows will assert. It could be aptly argued that

> Forrest Reid's books have attracted—and still attract—a small but loyal readership; small because of the undoubted "limitation" of his chosen subject, and loyal because of the unfailing clarity and style with which he treated it. His recurrent themes—childhood, youth and the loss of innocence—in some sense reflect the limitation of his appeal but might also, in part at least, explain the allegiance of his readers.[3]

However, it could be argued instead that this "limitation" resides not with Reid's subject but with the self-contained nature of his writing, a claim made in an anonymous article in the *Times Literary Supplement* in 1953:

> Forrest Reid's self-sufficiency, as man and writer, won for him a small, loyal body of like-minded friends and readers. This same quality, rather than any self-imposed restriction of theme, has lim-

ited his following and allowed him to be esteemed as a "specialist" novelist writing for a very small, esoteric minority.[4]

Or, as Reid himself suggests, this "limitation" may reside with the reading public:

> Both ancient philosopher and modern poet throw their net among the stars, and capture a strange and wandering loveliness that will always seem unearthly and illusive to those who, consciously or unconsciously, have accepted materialism, and to those upon whose souls the practical cares of life have closed down like a coffin-lid.[5]

Whatever the cause of this neglect, Reid is indeed, as Paul Goldman variously defines him: "a writer, scholar and collector who has inexplicably and unjustifiably slipped from view"—"a writer who [. . .] warrants both revaluation and rediscovery"—"a novelist and an autobiographer [who] is almost without peer, in his innate grasp of the complex feelings and emotions engendered by male adolescence."[6]

The distinctiveness of Forrest Reid, as an author, resides in his "mapping of the lost demesnes of childhood,"[7] in his unique perception and presentation of adolescence as "a place to dream the sleepy hours away! a place suggestive of, leading to, that inner contemplative life, to the boy, even then, so precious!"[8] Given the contemplative nature of his various works, they were not meant to be read only once, then pushed aside and forgotten, for *remembrance* is their essence, which is equally true of the cameo before us, for it is enwrapped in a belief that "even the memory of a single rapturous hour," as Reid relates, "is better than years passed in untroubled shadow."[9] This appreciation for a Blakean "eternity in an hour" is evident in all of Reid's works, and *The Garden God* is no exception.

The Garden God: A Tale of Two Boys was first published by David Nutt, in London, in November 1905, roughly a month after Reid had belatedly arrived at the University of Cambridge as a thirty-year-old undergraduate. Produced in an exquisite edition bound in vellum and gold, *The Garden God* was only Reid's second novel, a novel for which he received, in lieu of royalties, twelve presentation copies. However, for Reid, this novel abounded in hopes that were personal and literary rather than monetary. Although he would later claim in *Apostate*, his first autobiography, that "out of fragments of the world I shared with others, out of scattered glimpses of the past, out of nature, and out of my own dreams and desires, I had built up this world which I did not and could not share"[10]—this self-assessment fails to acknowledge that there had indeed been a time when he had hoped, perhaps naïvely, to share those dreams and their attendant desires in a fashion that would have been uncommonly bold, as well as to herald his own arrival as a writer of thinly disguised, autobiographical romance.

Had it retained its original dedication (complete with its envoy),[11] a dedication directed to his beloved friend Andrew Rutherford, *The Garden God* would have achieved both of those ends:

DEDICATION

My little love tale
I offer to you now;
So slight a thing,
So full of garden scents and flowers
And noise of running water,
Yet deep as secret lives—
For I have strewn before my Garden God,
And on his brow and on his pedestal,
Flowers that once blossomed in my soul and yours—
That dropped to us
From the wide opened door of heaven;
And I have told,
In every little sound of leaf and bird
And softly splashing stream,
Of nothing but my love
Of nothing but my love for you, dear boy,
Who walk within my garden evermore.

ENVOY

When you have closed this book, lean back and dream
Of him who made it, and the tender love
He had for you: and how in every word
He wrote of these two boys that love did seem
To be foreshadowed, till at last above
The lonely silence of his life he heard
The god that spoke to bid his dream come true.

This dedication was as daring as could be—especially in 1905. However, for various, certainly explicable reasons, Reid replaced the above with a seemingly innocuous alternative:

TO
HENRY JAMES
THIS SLIGHT TOKEN
OF RESPECT
AND ADMIRATION

About this discretionary decision, Colin Cruise writes: "Had Reid published the original dedication his reputation would have suffered eternally. He would have allied himself to that band of writers producing Uranian stories and poetry—that genre of Romantic, almost chivalric, homosexual literature. As a consequence his literary career would have been bound to the confines of the private press or the limited edition."[12] Cruise's use of the word "homosexual" here is rather misleading, for the Uranians were *not* writers of what would commonly be considered "homosexual literature." The Uranians were, more precisely, writers of "pederastic literature," and the word "pederastic" aptly describes both Reid's desires and his artistry, a crucial fact, however disconcerting, with which Brian Taylor begins and ends his critical study of the author, *The Green Avenue: The Life and Writings of Forrest Reid, 1875-1947*:

> There is no doubt that Reid's sexual inclinations—he liked small boys—have been a major reason for this reticence, but undoubtedly Reid's pederasty, idealised and frustrated though it largely was, is an important factor—some would say the crucial one—in any interpretation of his life or appreciation of his work. The two are

related in a particularly transparent way. Whereas, for example, Henry James might attempt to disguise his personality in, or beneath, his chosen style, Forrest Reid's obsessions—no other word will do—show clearly through all of his writing. Forrest Reid loved boys, wrote about boys, and wanted to write about nothing else. His inclinations, albeit sexual in origin, found expression in all of his opinions and ideas, on literature and on life.[13]

Forrest Reid's obsession was with boys and with boyhood, with their fictional representation and with its literary recall. Any appreciation of his life and writing must do more than take this fact into account; it must begin with it. That Reid was a pederast is of course one explanation, but of itself the fact imparts little understanding. [However,] the boys of Reid's imagination—Denis Bracknel, Peter Waring, Grif Weston, Beach Traill, and above all, Tom Barber, although they often talk in a style and with a wisdom mature beyond their years are all carefully desensualised characters.[14]

Even if his recognisable pederasty remained *only* on the level of desire—for "if there can be such a thing as a puritanical pederast," writes Taylor, "Forrest Reid was that person"[15]—Reid nonetheless appreciated that bountiful dangers accompanied any revelation of such desires, as in publishing that intimate dedication to Andrew Rutherford, a dedication that "would have allied [him] to that band of writers producing Uranian stories and poetry." Those dangers arose because, even among the university educated of his day, same-sex desire, in any of its manifestations, was beyond the pale of consideration, perhaps even mention, hence truly warranting the dub Lord Alfred Douglas had bestowed upon it more than a decade before: "The Love That Dare Not Speak Its Name."[16] This is aptly illustrated by a private note that E. M. Forster made in his commonplace book:

Mowbray Morris, editor of *Macmillan's Magazine*, to an undergraduate friend at Cambridge, January, 1886:

I still keep and always shall keep to my theory that it is not fair to lump all the Greeks together under one hideous ban. Nothing will ever persuade me that the best Greeks of the best time deserved such an imputation. There are of course some desperate passages in Plato, which it is impossible to get over. But then, Plato was not quite of the best time. The decadence had begun when he wrote; and moreover he always wrote impersonally, dramatically. But men such as Aeschylus, Sophocles, Phidias: they could not have done the work they did had they used a vice which must degrade a man all over, intellectually as well as morally:

> Not from a vain or shallow thought
> His awful Jove young Phidias brought.

Still less from a bestial one. "Oh that my lot may lead me in the path of holy innocence—" Sophocles wrote that . . . a Pagan. You cannot tell me that the man who wrote those words was—well, what we need not name.[17]

Such was a liberal, even educated opinion from 1886. However, Oscar Wilde's trials would, a decade later, significantly alter the reception of such opinions, both for the educated and for the general public.

Wilde, who had always praised "feasting with panthers,"[18] was caught in a descending, moralistic cage, a cage crafted legally by the Labouchère addition to the Criminal Law Amendment Act of 1885 (48 & 49 Victoria, c.69), legislation that extended, exponentially, the criminality of same-sex erotic practices—[19]

Any male person who, in public or private, commits, or is a party to the commission of, or procures or attempts to procure the commission by any male person of, any act of gross indecency with another male person, shall be guilty of a misdemeanour, and, being convicted thereof, shall be liable, at the discretion of the Court, to be imprisoned for any term not exceeding two years with or without hard labour.[20]

—a cage crafted emotively by the Cleveland Street Scandal of 1889, which exposed a "rent-boy" ring at 19 Cleveland Street, in London's West End, a sort of "telegraph-boy brothel" frequented by gentlemen and aristocrats.[21] Although the Criminal Law Amendment Act greatly reduced the severity of a criminal conviction—which had formerly involved a lengthy imprisonment spanning from ten years to life—such a conviction, even when it led to police supervision rather than imprisonment, inevitably spelled one's doom as far as reputation, career, and relationships were concerned—even when one was not as famous as an Oscar Wilde. A conviction for committing "an act of gross indecency" was, for the Victorians and the Edwardians, equivalent to the brand of Cain. However, the implications of the Labouchère addition were far more encompassing than just for "sodomy": this legislation provided a legal instrument for overt and covert surveillance into all areas of illicit sexual behaviour—hence its dub, "the Blackmailer's Charter."

This was the environment in which those with homoerotic and/or pederastic desires found themselves cowering, however defiantly, after 1885. This environment was especially dangerous for the Uranians, a group of poets, artists, and prose writers who constituted a vague "fellowship of pederasts" in England between roughly 1858 and 1930, a group who celebrated pederastic love and its attendant pedagogical practices, practices tracing back—or so the Uranians liked to assert, however histrionically—to ancient Greece. This group's first "declaration" was a collection of verses titled *Ionica*, "a classic paean to romantic paiderastia"[22] published by the Eton master William Johnson (*later* Cory) in 1858.[23] However, the Uranian movement—though "movement" may be far too formal a demarcation for such a clandestine group—would later find itself under other masters: Walter Pater, a Fellow of Brasenose College, Oxford, and the "High Priest of the Decadents";[24] and, to a lesser extent, John Addington Symonds, ever a disciple of Johnson.[25] As protégés of Benjamin Jowett, Regius Professor of Greek at Oxford and the pre-eminent Victorian translator of Plato, both Pater and Symonds became virtuosos of the evasive, Platonic style that would soon become the hallmark of Uranian writing, for it accommodated and facilitated a textual, voyeuristic posturing—a proximity to the object of desire without that distance being defeated, at least artistically—a unique style in English letters that suited their decadent temperaments, both aesthetically and psychologically. Over time, the Uranians became proficient in employing this style to convey dangerous, often pederastic subtexts, prompting Wilde to warn, rather playfully, in his (in)famous "Preface" to *The Picture of Dorian Gray*:

All art is at once surface and symbol.
Those who go beneath the surface do so at their peril.
Those who read the symbol do so at their peril.[26]

However, with his usual hubris, Wilde failed to anticipate that his own apologia for "The Love That Dare Not Speak Its Name"—delivered in the dock of the Old Bailey in 1895—would become the death knell for this suggestive, eroticised style of indirection, an indirection that had already begun to peter out with Symonds's death in 1893, and Pater's in 1894. In essence, the brilliantly opaque and multifaceted language of the early Uranians was replaced thereafter with turbulent directness, a directness that eventually infiltrated the language of law, psychology, journalism, and the street, a directness that encouraged simplistic taxonomies such as "the homosexual" and "the invert."

Further, Wilde's trials nullified most, if not all, of the aesthetic, educational, and other capital that the Uranians had amassed over decades by discreetly circulating pamphlets, poems, essays, paintings, and photographic "studies." These trials also dampened the Uranian hope of exercising a broader cultural influence through periodicals such as the *Artist and Journal of Home Culture*, which tactfully printed Uranian material until Charles Kains Jackson resigned his editorship in 1894 (a serendipitous decision, given that, a year later, it would have been untenable to circulate Uranian material so openly).

Because of Wilde's trials—which resulted in "the sacrifice of male homosexuality to male homophobia"[27]—it suddenly became far too dangerous for a Uranian apologist such as Edward Carpenter to include an essay like "Homogenic Love: and Its Place in a Free Society" in his collection *Love's Coming-of-Age* (1896). Carpenter phrased this as: "The Wilde trial had done its work; and silence must henceforth reign on sex-subjects."[28] For the next decade, the "silence" that Carpenter forecasted remained—that is, until 1908, when he broke that silence himself by publishing *The Intermediate Sex: A Study of Some Transitional Types of Men and Women*, the first volume in English that, despite validating same-sex desire, garnered a wide readership.

Because it was lavishly published in 1905, during that vitriolic "decade of silence," Forrest Reid's slender volume *The Garden God* becomes all the more a display of daring—perhaps even recklessness—the sort of daring one might expect from the likes of Reid's equally pederastic contemporary, T. E. Lawrence. However, Reid was no Lawrence of Arabia; and, for whatever reason, romantic or discretionary, he decided, perhaps insightfully, that fronting his *Garden God* with a dedication and an envoy extended to his beloved Andrew was simply too confrontational to be tenable.

Like E. M. Forster, that friend he shared in common with Lawrence, Forrest Reid was also clearly contemplating "Where Angels Fear to Tread" in 1905, though he would venture into that decadent realm less scandalously and perhaps less erotically than would Forster's protagonist Lilia Herriton, ever accompanied by her young Italian. However, Reid's willingness to *dare* (in all the resonances of that word) was not simply a feature of his pressing desire for Andrew Rutherford, or of his novel about two schoolboys, or of this particular year: his entire life displays a constant, though cautious treading of a singularly dangerous, pederastic path, as one might expect from a writer for whom "The Greek Anthology was in his bones"[29] and for whom the title of his second autobiography was *Private Road*.

For Reid, there was no distinction between the discreet and the discrete, a verity that he had gleaned from his reading of Pater, who had elevated this merging into a cardinal virtue: *ascêsis*. In his "Preface" to *The Renaissance*, Pater glosses this favoured concept as "the austere and serious girding of the loins in youth,"[30] a girding that suggests rigorous self-control, self-discipline, and self-mastery. Perhaps Reid's life illustrates this degree of *ascêsis*, perhaps it does not; however, in order to evaluate this, one must brush aside the traditional claim that "Forrest Reid lived a simple, indeed a humdrum life. Oddly enough, that is the only biographical fact about him that need have significance for literary critics."[31]

"Forrest Reid, 1875-1947": A Life in Cameo

> Deeper and deeper he sank into his thoughts. He supposed it
> was true that it took a long time really to get to know people,
> and that he was always in too great a hurry. Certainly he was
> in too great a hurry to tell them he liked them, and it hadn't
> answered well in the past.
>
> —Forrest Reid, from *Uncle Stephen*[32]

Rarely has a writer of this calibre had so cameo a life, a life framed,
rather hermetically, within the confines of Belfast, in what is now
Northern Ireland, where he was born on 24 June 1875, at 20 Mount
Charles. He was born the last child of Robert Reid, a middle-class
Irish merchant who died six years after Forrest's birth, and Frances
Matilda Reid, *née* Parr, an English aristocrat whose lineage, according to *Burke's Peerage*, reached back to the family of Kather-
ine Parr, Henry VIII's most fortunate of wives, and Ann Parr, the
wife of the Earl of Pembroke whose grandson is short-listed as the
original for Shakespeare's beloved "Mr. W. H." However impres-
sive Frances Reid's lineage, it had failed to translate into financial
stability; and, amidst declining fortunes, fortunes soon to fall even
further because of the death of Robert Reid, the family was forced
to migrate to no. 15, a smaller house across the street.

Although Reid's childhood was rarely idyllic, it was nonetheless bountiful in formative tensions, many of which sprang from
his own prodigal individuality. His childhood response to religion
is illustrative of this. Reared in the Church of Ireland, Reid developed an early antipathy to Christianity (and later to formal reli-
gions *en masse*), an antipathy that lasted a lifetime:

> I hated Sunday, I hated church, I hated Sunday School, I hated Bi-
> ble stories, I hated everybody mentioned in both the Old and New
> Testaments, except perhaps the impenitent thief, Eve's snake, and
> a few similar characters. And I never disguised these feelings. From
> dawn till sunset the day of rest was for me a day of storm and bat-
> tle, renewed each week, and carried on for years with a pertinacity
> that now seems hardly credible, till at length the opposition was
> exhausted and I was allowed to go my own way.[33]

From the age of eleven, Reid began to attend Miss Hardy's Prep School, in Cliftonpark, then later The Royal Belfast Academical Institution. Given his family's fallen fortunes, Reid had no choice but to pursue a profession, and he was subsequently apprenticed to Henry Musgrave, a tea-merchant. Soon after beginning this apprenticeship, he was asked to supervise an even newer arrival, Andrew Rutherford, an assignment that quickly broadened beyond tea and its transport: "It was, of course, first love; and Andrew and Forrest began to spend most of their free time together."[34] In February 1896—although less than a year after Wilde's sensational trials—Reid felt emboldened enough to show Andrew several intimate passages from his private journal, passages that elucidated the nature of his desire for Andrew. This tense and tantalising scene provides the climax for Reid's *Apostate*, an autobiography that chronicles his life till that crucial moment:

> For the first time I had admitted someone to my secret world, to my innermost thoughts. . . .
> Already he must have crossed the threshold. In the quiet of the room I could hear no sound but now and then the rustle of a page when he turned it. For an instance I glanced at him. His face was a little flushed, his dark hair tumbled down over his forehead. But I turned away quickly and did not look back. I sat waiting, trying now to shut out every thought from my mind. . . .
> The time slowly drew on: half an hour, nearly an hour must have gone by. The window grew darker and darker, and presently I knew that in a little, a very little while, the reading must come to an end. Then the silence seemed all at once to grow so intense that I felt nothing could ever again break it.[35]

Several years passed, during which Reid, in this idiosyncratic novitiate in Belfast, developed a degree of mastery in the subtle arts of love, the tea-trade, and the novel.

In 1903, "as Andrew's affection began to wane," suggests Brian Taylor, "Forrest found friends in both of the other Rutherford brothers, James and William."[36] From these identical twins, it was James who would, in many ways, supplant Andrew in Reid's affection. However, the story is far more complicated than that. For one thing, Andrew had begun to appreciate more fully the societal implications of this "affection," an affection that, at the very least, bordered on "The Love That Dare Not Speak Its Name." Andrew became increasingly uneasy about how this "affection" would be perceived and responded to by those on the outside, since it bespoke, however partially, a form of love, intimacy, and/or erotic expression that society's "legitimate" powers—social, medical, ethical, religious, legal, political, scholarly, and familial—deemed maladjusted, psychotic, immoral, sinful, unlawful, fringe, objectionable, and/or intrusive. This concern surfaces in a letter to Reid in December 1903, a letter written after Andrew had read several chapters of his friend's evolving schoolboy romance, *The River*.[37]

> Can an Ethiopian change his spots? No more can I alter my nature, and to avoid any future disappointment on your part, I may as well assure you that I have not the slightest intention of chucking up the law and wandering disconsolate through the world [. . .][38]

Andrew's last statement—"I have not the slightest intention of chucking up the law and wandering disconsolate through the world"—has the fate of Wilde writ large as its context. To his credit, Reid seems not to have pressured Andrew further in this regard, though one must assume that, given the comments above, Andrew was less than pleased by the intimacy developing between Reid and his younger brother James, especially since James seems to have had neither his brother's scruples in this regard nor perhaps a need to "alter [his] nature" to accord with Reid's swelling "affection."

Over the next few years, Forrest Reid, ever in the company of the Rutherford twins, reworked the contents of that never-to-be-finished novel, *The River*, the result being two novels that are similar in theme: *The Kingdom of Twilight* (published by T. Fisher Unwin in 1904) and *The Garden God: A Tale of Two Boys* (published by David Nutt in 1905).

In October 1905, bastioned by a small legacy left to him by his mother, Forrest Reid, now at the tender age of thirty, began his academic career—at Christ's College, Cambridge. Reid remained at Cambridge for the next three years, the result succinctly described by Taylor: "Reid gained a second-class degree and left Cambridge little wiser than before. He gained one life-long friend [Theodore Bartholomew] with whom he could remain on terms of complete confidence, but he never went back. He returned to the north of Ireland and stayed there for the rest of his life."[39]

Meanwhile, his affection for James Rutherford continued, and they toured Europe together in 1907, 1908, and 1911. In fact, not long after his return from Cambridge, Reid and James began to share a residence, at 9 South Parade—from whence, in 1914, they would move together to 12 Fitzwilliam Avenue. While Taylor asserts that "there is no reason to suppose that the relationship between Forrest Reid and James Rutherford was in any way a homosexual one,"[40] evidence from another quarter makes this assertion less convincing. One of Reid's confidants, E. M. Forster, made the following entry in his private commonplace book:

> *Osbert Burdett's death* has its usual effect on me. That is to say here is a man whom I do not respect or care for or know well, and suppose that I shall see from time to time at a committee meeting. He slips on a moving staircase and dies of the injuries. His unimportance reminds me that he might be anyone. He went to my preparatory school after I left it, followed me to King['s College, Cambridge] ditto, wrote some faint and fretful essays, tried to get off with Forrest Reid in the lavatory of the Savile Club, became [a Roman Catholic], feebly denigrated Goldie, had to marry the housemaid, worried Mrs Hardy about blue vinney cheese, and God knows why he was elected to the committee of the [London Library] to represent literature alongside of Desmond [MacCarthy] & myself. I have not a charitable thought about him, nor a vehement one, yet his absence frightens me, I keep on hoping he didn't suffer.[41]

This passing detail—that Burdett "tried to get off with Forrest Reid in the lavatory of the Savile Club"—is curiously phrased, and appears less a declined erotic proposition than a moment thwarted by the intrusion of a third party or a lack of sustained arousal. Whatever one decides about this episode at the Savile, the Forrest Reid of this private note resembles little the "Forrest Reid [who] did not," according to Taylor, "like homosexuals; in fact, he rather despised them. More precisely, he disliked homosexuality that *showed*. In fact, he considered the sexual act itself degrading. He disapproved of fulfilled homosexuality and was disgusted by the idea of fulfilled heterosexuality."[42] As is so typical for biography, there is much here that needs explaining, much to which we are simply not privy.

Meanwhile, "Reid's domestic arrangements had 'fallen into a tranquil routine' over the last eight years and there must have seemed little reason to expect matters to alter very much; so that when James Rutherford announced, at the age of thirty-six, that he intended to marry, the news must have come as an unwelcome shock."[43] As if seeking, in melodramatic fashion, for a space that would mirror his desolation, Reid moved in 1917 to 62 Dublin Road, just opposite a factory in a busy industrial district, the sort of place he would have found repulsive on every level.

Although it did not lead to a permanent domestic relationship, this period with James Rutherford coincided, for Reid, with the forging of a number of permanent literary relationships. Perhaps surprisingly, given that he remained in Belfast, his literary sphere now encompassed several individuals of note, though these friendships rarely broadened beyond letters and infrequent visits. While it is true that *The Bracknels: A Family Chronicle* (published by Edward Arnold in 1911) occasioned his friendships with E. M. Forster and Walter de la Mare, even friendships with such as these proved incapable of motivating him to participate, in any significant way, in literary circles, even those of his fellow Uranians in London, Oxford, or his alma mater. In fact, in his critical study of Yeats, published only a few years later, Reid asserts: "Great art is essentially lonely. [. . .] The work that counts is more likely to be conceived in a rectory on the Yorkshire moors, or in a cottage in the lake country, than in the self-conscious atmosphere of literary circles."[44] So Reid remained in "provincial" Belfast, in his own version of a Brontëan or Wordsworthian seclusion, a seclusion in which he produced much: *Following Darkness* (1912), *The Gentle Lover: A Comedy of Middle Age* (1913), *W. B. Yeats: A Critical Study* (1915), and *At the Door of the Gate* (1915).

In 1916, prior to moving to the noisy seclusion of Dublin Road, Reid met a twelve-year-old schoolboy in Belvoir Park, in south Belfast—Kenneth Hamilton. Hamilton, whose family lived near Fitzwilliam Avenue, quickly became "his devoted prodigy": "The boy adored the older man, [who then] used, even exploited, his unquestioning friendship to justify his part in it."[45] Around Hamilton—who served as the muse for much of *The Spring Song* (1916)—Reid wove a far more pederastic world than he had hitherto known, a world far more agreeable to himself. This "weaving" is evident in the nine issues of *Kenneth's Magazine* (appearing at intervals between 1917 and 1919), a periodical that, although each instalment was "published" in only a single handwritten copy, was nonetheless bountiful in textual and pictorial contributions by Hamilton, Reid, and a number of their friends. During this blissful period, Reid also wrote *A Garden by the Sea: Stories and Sketches* (1918), *Pirates of the Spring* (1919), and *Pender Among the Residents* (1922).

Reid and Kenneth Hamilton remained particularly intimate until this "fair boy," now sixteen, enlisted in the Merchant Service, partly on Reid's prompting. The rest of the tale is a tragic one, as Taylor relates:

> Kenneth spent the next two years sailing around the world. He did not have a happy time at sea. In Australia, he spent some time cattle ranching, and during this time Forrest and Kenneth exchanged affectionate letters. But gradually, Kenneth's letters grew fewer and eventually stopped. One Christmas, a pudding sent to Kenneth was returned alive with maggots. And then, finally, a letter was returned unopened and stamped with one word, "deceased."[46]

As Reid would explain more than a decade later: "The last news of [Kenneth], received from strangers, was that he had ridden out alone one day into the Australian bush. From that ride he did not return, and no trace of what had happened was ever discovered."[47]

In 1924, Forrest Reid decided to move away from dismal Dublin Road—a place made all the more dismal because of its residual associations with Kenneth Hamilton, who was still then alive and sending back occasional letters and poems from Australia. Partly through the intervention of his friends, Reid moved into 13 Ormiston Crescent, at Knock, on the outskirts of Belfast, a house where he lived until his death (and which now bears a plaque to his memory, unveiled in 1952). This semi-detached council house, with its two small bedrooms, a study, kitchen and bathroom, became the private sphere—near to bursting with books—where he entertained his friends, most of whom would never have appreciated anything he had authored. These friends, most of whom were far from literary, were chosen by criteria as distinct as the man, a man who preferred the simple pleasures of bridge and croquet and jigsaws, of collecting stamps and old woodcuts. In essence, Ormiston Crescent became his Messolonghi, a field where one might expect to find him huddled over toy soldiers, a prized remnant of his childhood: "[As a child,] my cities were Greece, Athens, and the Peloponnesian States, and they were peopled by a military crowd, for there had come down to me from older brothers many armies of leaden soldiers."[48]

Ormiston Crescent was also blessedly bountiful in boys, a detail that is noted in passing by Russell Burlingham—"[Reid] used to enjoy the casual contacts he made with youngsters in the neighbourhood"[49]—though Burlingham fails, rather naïvely, to recognise the decadent potential of this, which is particularly noticeable in the following description, a description that becomes all the more salacious when one remembers Reid's pederastic bent: "Late in life, when he was over fifty, he suddenly started to collect stamps. [. . .] One of the great advantages of stamp-collecting was the opportunity it gave him of meeting small boys on equal terms."[50]

Reid's neighbours were not oblivious to his obvious desires, as is evident in a less naïve comment that constitutes the first paragraph of Norman Vance's essay "The Necessity of Forrest Reid":

> My mother knew Forrest Reid in the inter-war years. At least, they both lived in Ormiston Crescent in suburban east Belfast at that time, he at no. 13 and she on the other side of the road at no. 20. "What was he like?" I once asked, only to be told that he was rather peculiar: friendly enough to the boys of the neighbourhood, but he definitely did not like little girls.[51]

As for "the boys of the neighbourhood": at Ballyhackamore House, in nearby Upper Newtownards Road, lived the Montgomery family, whose grandson Desmond became one of Reid's lingering fascinations, as he himself admits: "Desmond was just the kind of boy I liked, toughish, self-reliant, fond of animals, and the best of pals."[52] Taylor succinctly summarizes this situation: "With new dogs for friends and new boys for companions, Forrest Reid settled comfortably into the house in Ormiston Crescent."[53]

So unlike his English friends, who would have found this atmosphere stiflingly provincial, Reid, in an encompassing cloud of pipe-smoke, found this atmosphere utterly inspiring, and here wrote his grandest works, including his masterpiece, a trilogy about a boy named Tom Barber—*Young Tom*, *The Retreat*, and *Uncle Stephen*.

While elaborating to Reid about his unfinished, homoerotic romance *Maurice*, E. M. Forster confessed: "One lives bottled up in a beautiful land of dreams. No more than a cocoon of frustrated desires, these dreams seem sometimes, something which I have spun round me to hide my love . . . and which cramps my power."[54] It was within just such a "cocoon"—this small home in Ormiston Crescent—that Reid would complete his *Apostate* (begun in 1923; published by Constable in 1926), an autobiography that chronicles his life into early manhood, an autobiography that ends with an account of that fateful episode in 1896 in which he bravely shared his intimate journal with his beloved Andrew Rutherford. This period in Ormiston Crescent was indeed a "cocoon," yet a cocoon that fostered nostalgic revels and creative incubation. Surrounded by his friends, his beloved pets, his even more beloved boys, and his memories, Reid experienced here the most productive period of his life.

The presence of Stephen Gilbert[55]—later himself a novelist as well as Reid's literary executor—can be credited for much of this. Gilbert, who was nineteen when he met Reid in 1931, soon became Reid's protégé and permanent friend, as well as an object of desire to rival even Andrew Rutherford and Kenneth Hamilton, both of whom remained ever malleable in Reid's vivacious memory. However, Gilbert seems never to have shared Reid's erotic desire, which positioned him, tauntingly, just out of reach, a position that proved beneficial for Reid as author, as Taylor so aptly explains:

"Desertion and unreciprocated, sometimes unsuspected, love, the inevitable pains of pederasty, nourished Reid's art and his response to his heart's deepest longings formed and developed his particular genius."[56]

A flurry of new novels took shape within this "cocoon of frustrated desires, these dreams": *Demophon: A Traveller's Tale* (1927), *Uncle Stephen* (1931), *Brian Westby* (1934), *The Retreat; or, The Machinations of Henry* (1936), and *Young Tom; or, Very Mixed Company* (1944). Two older novels—*Following Darkness* and *The Bracknels: A Family Chronicle*—were transformed to such a degree that Reid expected each "to be regarded as a new book": *Peter Waring* (1937) and *Denis Bracknel* (published posthumously in 1947). A number of critical volumes were newly written, or else compiled from lesser materials that had been written over decades: *Illustrators of the Sixties* (1928), *Walter de la Mare: A Critical Study* (1929), *Retrospective Adventures* (1940), *Notes and Impressions* (1942), *Poems from the Greek Anthology* (Reid's translations, published in 1943), and *The Milk of Paradise: Some Thoughts on Poetry* (1946). And a more encompassing and linear autobiography was completed—*Private Road* (1940). Although, under these conditions, his artistry acquired its greatest maturation and actualisation, few critics and readers noticed, to the puzzlement of Reid, who was edging towards seventy.

Although his novel *Brian Westby* had been widely praised in the press, substantially enhancing his reputation—although James S. Sleator and J. Arthur Greeves had both painted his portrait (the first now residing in the Ulster Museum; the second, in The Royal Academical Institution, Belfast)—although he had received an honorary doctorate from Queen's University, Belfast—although his novel *Young Tom* had been awarded the James Tait Black Memorial Prize, recognising it as the best piece of fiction published in 1944—Reid died "disappointed that he had not received the recognition he felt he deserved, but confident that he would be better treated in the fullness of time."[57] Reid's confidence seems, sixty years after his death from a disease of the spinal cord, to have been misplaced.

Despite his sixteen novels, his two autobiographies, and his other works, few then, and perhaps even fewer now, would consider his death—on 4 January 1947, at Warrenpoint, on the coast of County Down—to warrant more than that headstone in Dundonald Cemetery, Knock, Belfast, on which is inscribed: "Forrest Reid, 1875-1947." However, a more befitting, though problematic epitaph would read: "Forrest Reid, 1875-1947, Uranian Author and Friend."

"Forrest Reid, the Uranian": Among His Fellows

> And all that did then attend and follow,
> Were silent with love,—as you now, Apollo,
>   With envy of my sweet pipings.
>   —P. B. Shelley, from "Hymn to Pan"[58]

There is indeed some truth to E. M. Forster's admission that "one lives bottled up in a beautiful land of dreams. No more than a cocoon of frustrated desires, these dreams seem sometimes." Reid's agreement with this is expressed by the passage from Heraclitus that he chose as the epigraph for his first autobiography, *Apostate*: "They that are awake have one world in common, but of the sleeping each turns aside into a world of his own." This "land of dreams" arose because, as Reid admits, "My life, from as far back as I can remember, was never lived wholly in the open. I mean that it had its private side, that there were things I saw, felt, heard, and kept to myself. There were thoughts I kept to myself, too; and above all dreams."[59] Russell Burlingham glosses this as:

> Only in his head did he lead a different—and most *unordinary*—existence. There were, he recollected long afterwards, two lives—"one the external life of . . . games, collections, and the rest of it; the other a private life haunted by visions of beauty and the longing for an ideal companion . . . and it never occurred to me to ask myself whether one were less real than the other."[60]

What Burlingham is characterising here is the tension between Reid's public and private selves, between the expressed and the silenced, between what Gerard Manley Hopkins labels "overthought" and "underthought," and Oscar Wilde "surface" and "symbol." This disparity between life and art, between the expressed and the silenced was something that the Uranians of the Victorian and Edwardian periods came, in time, to appreciate and to make the cornerstone of their art. In Reid's case, this disparity was equally stark, which meant that life in Ulster promised much the same "limitation" as life anywhere else, London included: hence, "Reid believed in and sought, in Belfast, to live in accordance with the spirit of Greek Mediterranean culture."[61] This decision—to live, though differently, in Belfast—led, particularly among the literati, to the charge that he was "provincial," a "provincialism" that was all the more enigmatic because it arose by choice.[62]

Perhaps it was fortunate that Reid preferred to remain in "the provinces" of the Imperial Rome of his day, for he hoped never to hear those apocryphal, dying words of Julian the Apostate, the last pagan Emperor of Rome, as he watched the grandeur of the ancient world crumbling beneath the puritanical advance of Christianity: *Vicisti, Galilæe*—or, "You have conquered, O Galilean."[63] With those words, Algernon Charles Swinburne begins his poem "Hymn to Proserpine," a poem best encapsulated in lines 35-36:

> Thou hast conquered, O pale Galilean; the world has
> grown grey from thy breath;
> We have drunken of things Lethean, and fed on the
> fullness of death.

For Forrest Reid, Julian's lament is commingled with a lingering scepticism about Pan's demise, a commingling that encapsulates a desire to escape from the constraints of the Judeo-Christian worldview and its attendant sorrows. It is this pagan impulse that inspired Reid—aptly dubbed by several critics, "The Pan of Ulster"—to title his first autobiography *Apostate* and to write neopagan pieces such as "Pan's Pupil" (1905), a tale included here as "Appendix One." In his private commonplace book, E. M. Forster acknowledges this connection between his friend's interest in Pan and his anti-Christian stance: "Other claimants to Satanic intimacy; the Pan school, petering out in [R. S.] Hichens and E. F. Benson. [Nathaniel] Hawthorne's *Marble Faun* an early specimen of it: and Forrest Reid."[64]

Although "the Pan school" was indeed "petering out" at the

time Forster wrote the above, the Arcadian god Pan nonetheless remained, well beyond the *fin de siècle*, a common cultural theme and a veritable protagonist in dozens of books, not to mention scores of poems and short stories.[65] Among the most memorable of these are: *The Great God Pan* (1894), a novella by Arthur Machen, a writer about whom Reid published an article in the *Nation and Athenaeum* in November 1921; *Pan, af Løitnant Thomas Glahns papirer* (1894) by the Norwegian author Knut Hamsun, a work that contributed to his winning the Nobel Prize in Literature in 1920; *Pan* (1895-99), a prominent journal of avant-garde art and literature founded by Richard Dehmel, Otto Julius Bierbaum, and Julies Meier-Graefe; *The Little White Bird* (1901) by J. M. Barrie, which marks the first appearance of the character Peter Pan; *The Horned Shepherd* (1904) by Edgar Jepson; "The Story of a Panic" (1904), a short story by E. M. Forster; *The Wind in the Willows* (1908) by Kenneth Grahame; *Pan's Garden: A Volume of Nature Stories* (1912) and "The Touch of Pan" in *Day and Night Stories* (1917), both by Algernon Blackwood; "The Tomb of Pan" (1915), a short prose-poem by Edward J. M. D. Plunkett, 18th Baron Dunsany, who would later publish *The Blessing of Pan* (1927), a novel. It is within this tradition that many of the works of Forrest Reid, "The Pan of Ulster," find their place, as Forster recognised.

"Claimant to Satanic intimacy," a member of "the Pan school," an "Apostate"—these, in combination, give some indication of the neo-paganism that Reid and his works exude. However, in Reid's case (though certainly not in his case only), this paganism comes coupled with something far less conventional: an erotic disposition that is expressed through an "elevated" form of pederasty, a pederasty that he displays, symbolically, through the relationship between Pan and any boy, fictive or fleshy, who wanders into his garden:

> "Little piper, do you know into whose kingdom you have strayed?" He who spoke was a man, no longer young, dark like some statue of dark bronze, and naked. His thick shaggy hair curled over his low forehead, his features were ill-formed, his ears pointed, but his eyes were gentle.

The boy clasped his hands about his knees. He shook his head. "I do not know," he made answer, "but I think you must be Pan."

"Did you not call me to you? Do not be afraid. I will not harm you. You are a human boy, and must live out your destiny. I will not keep you. Someday, however, when the world seems very hard and cold, you will perhaps seek again the door to my fairyland, and if you find it then and enter, it will be to stay for ever and ever. You are a child, and I am very old, yet I will be here when you return."[66]

In similar fashion, the occasional boy found his way into the garden of "The Pan of Ulster," a kingdom such as Dublin Road or Ormiston Crescent where a young Kenneth Hamilton or Desmond Montgomery or Stephen Gilbert could "seek again the door to [. . .] fairyland." Given the above, it should come as no surprise that, despite his "provincialism," Forrest Reid became a recognisable member of the Uranians, that "fellowship of pederasts" whose literary and cultural history is chronicled by only two books—Timothy d'Arch Smith's *Love in Earnest: Some Notes on the Lives and Writings of English 'Uranian' Poets from 1889 to 1930*, and my own *Secreted Desires: The Major Uranians: Hopkins, Pater and Wilde*.

As one might expect, the Uranian theme that one finds in Reid's life also abounds in his works, a theme that his immediate contemporaries were cognisant of, occasionally alluding to it in a muted, tactful fashion:

Forrest Reid's theme is that a boy's open enjoyment of the natural world—its sights and sounds and colours, the warmth of the sun and the independence of animals, the sparkle of the sea and the smoothness of human bodies—persists into and beyond middle age, beneath thickening layers of pretence and apparent indifference.[67]

However, it should be kept in mind that Reid was writing within the distinctly "elevated" tradition of Victorian and Edwardian pederastic literature, a tradition first expressed in William Johnson's *Ionica*, a tradition that gained its fullest voice in works such as Walter Pater's *Plato and Platonism*, which cogently elucidates the Grecian passion that inspires this form of pederasty:

Brothers, comrades, who could not live without each other, they were the most fitting patrons of a place in which friendship, comradeship, like theirs, came to so much. Lovers of youth they remained, those enstarred types of it, arrested thus at that moment of miraculous good fortune as a consecration of the clean, youthful friendship, "passing even the love of woman," which [. . .] elaborated into a kind of art, became an elementary part of [ancient Greek] education. [. . .] The beloved and the lover, side by side through their long days of eager labour, and above all on the battlefield, became respectively, *aitês*, the hearer, and *eispnêlas*, the inspirer; the elder inspiring the younger with his own strength and noble taste in things.[68]

This "elevated" tradition found its antithesis in the blatantly "carnal" tradition later established by Pater's former disciple Oscar Wilde[69]—for, as Gerald Monsman explains, Wilde's tradition is based on "seductive (mis)constructions of Paterian aesthetic theories."[70]

Pater's tradition, in its purer form, suited Reid far better than Wilde's, especially if Taylor is correct in his assertion that "if there can be such a thing as a puritanical pederast, Forrest Reid was that person." Such a pederastic positionality is also at the heart of the following, written by Terence Hanbury White, a novelist who would, a decade after Reid's death, walk the same "elevated" Uranian path with a boy named Zed:

I have fallen in love with Zed. [. . .] It would be unthinkable to make Zed unhappy with the weight of this impractical, unsuitable love. It would be against his human dignity. Besides, I love him for being happy and innocent, so it would be destroying what I loved. He could not stand the weight of the world against such feelings—not that they are bad in themselves. It is the public opinion which makes them so. In any case, on every score of his happiness, not my safety, the whole situation is an impossible one. All I can do is to behave like a gentleman. It has been my hideous fate to be born with an infinite capacity for love and joy with no hope of using them.

I do not believe that some sort of sexual relations with Zed would do him harm—he would probably think and call them *t'rific*. I do not think I could hurt him spiritually or mentally. I do

not believe that perverts are made so by seduction. I do not think
that sex is evil, except when it is cruel or degrading, as in rape,
sodomy, etc., or that I am evil or that he could be. But the practical facts of life are an impenetrable barrier—the laws of God,
the laws of Man. His age, his parents, his self-esteem, his self-reli-
ance, the progress of his development in a social system hostile to
the heart, the brightness of his being which has made this what a
home should be for three whole weeks of utter holiday, the fact
that the old exist for the benefit of the young, not vice versa, the
factual impossibilities set up by law and custom, the unthinkable-
ness of turning him into a lonely or sad or eclipsed or furtive person—every possible detail of what is expedient, not what is moral,
offers the fox to my bosom, and I must let it gnaw.[71]

White's conclusion—that "the practical facts of life are an impenetrable barrier [. . .] [that] offers the fox to my bosom, and I must
let it gnaw"—is analogous to the "elevated" Uranian stance advocated by Walter Pater and perhaps more stringently by another of
his disciples, the poet Lionel Johnson, as Linda Dowling explains:

> Yet the most radical claim of the new Uranian poetry [represented
> by writers like Lionel Johnson] would always be that it sang the
> praises of a mode of spiritual and emotional attachment that was,
> at some ultimate level, innocent or asexual.

> The great significance of [Lionel] Johnson's work as a Uranian
> poet thus becomes his attempt to defend the older tradition of
> pederastic Hellenism in the face of the newer sexual realism in
> male love being asserted in the early 1890s by such writers as Sy-
> monds and [Theodore] Wratislaw and indeed by [Lord Alfred]
> Douglas himself.[72]

Given Dowling's comments, it is noteworthy that, in *The Irishman*
in March 1916, Reid published a review (signed "R.F.") titled "The
Poetical Works of Lionel Johnson." Reid fully appreciated that the
"elevated" Uranian tradition advocated by Pater and Lionel Johnson was his own.

Further, there is evidence beyond the literary that allies Reid
with the Uranians, evidence more tangibly biographical. In fact, if
one were to make a short-list of the *fin de siècle* pederastic clique

in Britain, that list would include Walter Pater, Lionel Johnson, Ronald Firbank, Theodore Bartholomew, Marc-André Raffalovich, Edmund Gosse, Edward Perry Warren, and Gleeson White—all of whom had some connection to the life of Forrest Reid.

While it can rightly be said that Pater's culture was directed towards "a small band of elite 'Oxonian' souls,"[73] that culture would find itself equally flourishing, by the time of his death, at the University of Cambridge, where Pater also had a following. Among his later Cambridge followers was Forrest Reid, who, like many of his contemporaries, arrived to Cambridge fully versed in the writings of Pater and his coterie, a decadent influence that is strikingly evident in his early novel *The Garden God*, a novel that is more of a tribute to the influence of Pater's masterpieces *The Renaissance* and *Marius the Epicurean*—as well as to lesser pieces such as "The Child in the House"—than to Henry James or Anatole France, two influences that are indeed present, though in a muted form. Like many of his fellow Uranians, Reid would continue to revel in a Paterian disposition long after he had jettisoned a Paterian style.

While at Cambridge, Reid met several fellow undergraduates who shared his Uranian tastes and Paterian disposition, such as Ronald Firbank, who had a "coy naughtiness about birches and pretty boys," and Theodore Bartholomew, who would later become an important, though fringe member of the Uranian circle, important for his rare Uranian collections and for writing a preliminary biography of Frederick Rolfe (Baron Corvo), one of the most prominent and certainly the most flamboyant of the Uranians. Bartholomew would later become a close friend of Charles Edward Sayle, a Uranian poet whose home in Cambridge served as a sort of Uranian salon.

Sayle and Bartholomew were also friends of Marc-André Raffalovich, a Uranian writer and socialite whose lover was John Henry Gray, Wilde's lover at the time of the publication of *The Picture of Dorian Gray*. Reid and Raffalovich would later become friends, mostly *via* letter. Much the same relationship developed between Reid and Edmund Gosse, a well-known man of letters whose literary friendships, over several decades, ranged from Walter Pater to Siegfried Sassoon, and whose love for the academic sculptor Hamo

Thornycroft allowed Lytton Strachey, with his usual, cheeky acerbity, to label him a "hamosexual."

Through Bartholomew or Raffalovich or Gosse, Reid seems to have become acquainted with Edward Perry Warren, a wealthy American expatriate who, after graduating from Harvard University, then Oxford, became the pre-eminent collector of antiquities of his day. Warren, who wrote under the pseudonym "Arthur Lyon Raile," was also one of the most outspoken of the Uranian poets, as well as the writer of the group's most elaborate apologia, his privately printed, three-volume *Defence of Uranian Love* (1928-30), the initial section of which is titled "The Boy-Lover." With his usual daring, Reid published, in the *Irish Statesman* in April 1928, an article on Warren's pseudonymous poetry titled "Pagan Poetry," an article he later reprinted as "Arthur Lyon Raile" in his *Retrospective Adventures* (1941). As a necessary aside, it should be mentioned that one of the co-authors of the first biography of Warren—*Edward Perry Warren: The Biography of a Connoisseur* (1941)—was none other than Osbert Burdett, noteworthy for trying "to get off with Forrest Reid in the lavatory of the Savile Club."

Among the Uranian types with whom Reid was on terms of close friendship was Sir Samuel Knox Cunningham, a future Unionist member of Parliament as well as a member of a decadent circle that, unofficially, procured young men "from institutions in Northern Ireland" and transported them "to orgies in London."[74] As with many of Reid's contacts, this friendship with Cunningham, which lasted for the rest of his life, draws into question the chaste nature of Reid's affections, such that one could simply posit that the lack of concrete evidence to the contrary tells more about Reid's sense of discretion than it does about anything else.

In his review of Brian Taylor's *The Green Avenue*, a review published in the *Times Literary Supplement* in February 1981, Francis King comments:

> Dr Taylor seems to believe—his book errs on the side of reticence and one cannot be certain—that Reid never achieved sexual congress with any of his boys. I myself doubt this, at least in the case of Kenneth Hamilton. [. . .] In the case of at least one other of

Reid's youthful friends, there is the probability that sexual inter-
course, however furtive and fumbling, also took place.[75]

In response to what he perceives to be King's "attempts to adjust
the received notion of Forrest Reid's private life," Alan Hollinghurst, in a letter to the editor of the *TLS*, immediately retorted:

> If only for the sake of biographical accuracy (not, after all, an un-
> serious consideration) any substantiated information about such
> private matters is of interest. Since, as far as I know, there is no
> published confirmation of what Mr King alleges, his manner of
> simply asserting it serves only to confuse the biographical impres-
> sion with rumour and speculation.[76]

To this, King responded with the following:

> Alan Hollinghurst would like me to be more explicit in my state-
> ments about Forrest Reid's private life. Biographical accuracy, he
> reminds us, is "not, after all, an unserious consideration." Unfor-
> tunately, the libel laws in this country are also not, after all, an
> unserious consideration. There I must, therefore, leave the mat-
> ter—at all events for the present.[77]

Whatever one decides about the (un)likelihood of Reid's "sexual congress with any of his boys," it is nonetheless clear that he
was fated to be amongst the Uranian "fellows," which was true
even on occasions that had nothing to do with their "fellowship"
or their shared erotic desires. A curious example of this is that, in
his teens, Reid had begun amassing what would become a rare collection of Victorian illustrations, most of which had been cut from
periodicals (a collection that he donated, in 1946, to the Ashmolean
Museum at Oxford). This "hobby" led, later in life, to his publication of *Illustrators of the Sixties* (1928), only the second authoritative
account on this topic, the first being *English Illustration: The Sixties*
(1897), written by Gleeson White. White, a prominent editor and
writer on art topics, has been described as follows:

> He was, however, much too canny to come into the open with
> his secret emotions [. . .] but he was undoubtedly enormously
> involved in Uranian matters, for in his library were to be found

> [many of the most prized and obscure Uranian treasures.] [. . .] In
> the first volume of the *Studio* [which he edited] is printed an essay
> on the male nude in photography which was almost certainly writ-
> ten by White himself, revealing him as an expert in this form of
> art. In the course of the article, he printed a photograph of Cecil
> Castle, nude, lying on his stomach, taken by Baron Corvo. [In fact,
> there was a] Gleeson White—Baron Corvo—Charles Kains Jack-
> son—Cecil Castle contingent of the Uranian movement [. . .][78]

One rarely escapes one's fate, and Reid's seems to have been that
of a Uranian fellow and author. As a result, he "spoke and wrote
with grave simplicity about a system of values which, if adopted,
would turn the world's ideas gently but firmly topsy-turvy."[79] One
of those for whom this "topsy-turvy" turn was more than disa-
greeable was, perhaps not surprisingly, Henry James.

The Garden God: An "Upsetting"

> How came it that these two, having each such a wealth of affec-
> tion to bestow, could not spend it on one another?
> —H. O. Sturgis, from *Tim*[80]

In 1891, Howard Overing Sturgis published an utterly saccharine
novel about a love affair between two Eton schoolboys—*Tim: A
Story of School Life*—about which Timothy d'Arch Smith writes:
"The importance of Sturgis's book lies in the fact that it was the
model on which the Irish novelist, Forrest Reid, based *The Garden
God* in 1905."[81] This detail makes Reid's choice of a replacement
dedication—"To Henry James / This Slight Token of Respect and
Admiration"—all the more curious, perhaps even serendipitous;
for, unbeknownst to him, James was, at that very moment, still
lingering in the afterglow of a loving relationship with Sturgis:

> During the first few years of the twentieth century it seems that
> Henry James fell briefly but passionately in love with Howard
> Sturgis, a love that Sturgis may have reciprocated. This was the
> love of a powerful older man for a younger socialite and writer
> who lacked James's own professional confidence and security, who
> sought from James support and reassurance regarding his writing.

[. . .] But as much as James desired companionship and love at this time in his life, he was unable to prevent himself from criticizing Sturgis's work freely, criticism that must have been wounding. The relationship lessened in intensity after 1904, and though toward the end of his life James expressed deep affection for Sturgis, the two never achieved a long-lasting bond.[82]

This description of Sturgis—"a younger [. . .] writer who lacked James's own professional confidence and security, who sought from James support and reassurance regarding his writing"—equally befits Reid at the time he made, in the phrasing of Thomas Chatterton, his "mistaken homage to an unknown God,"[83] in this case to Henry James, "the Master."

Despite its obvious similarity to Sturgis's *Tim* (or perhaps because of this), the further James read in *The Garden God*, the more disturbed he became. He would undoubtedly have revoked his permission for the dedication had he known beforehand that Reid's second novel would champion "a Hellenised version of pederastic love."[84] Clearly disturbed by its "unmistakable note of eroticism,"[85] James wrote an acerbic letter to Reid, a letter that represents—because its recipient destroyed it—a permanent lacuna, an impossibility to judge the exact reasoning and tone of James's response. All that can be known for certain is that, in Reid's words, "the Master was not pleased."[86]

Perhaps the best explanation for James's reaction, whatever it was, can be found in a private note made by E.M. Forster: "[Henry James] in *The Turn of the Screw* is merely declining to think about homosex, and the knowledge that he is declining throws him into the necessary fluster."[87] Reid had indeed been an avid reader of James, a reader who was especially appreciative of the James who had written *The Turn of the Screw* and "The Pupil," a short story from which Reid's third novel, *The Bracknels*, seems to have sprung, at least in part. However, "the Master was not pleased"—so strikingly "not pleased" that he desired no further association, under any circumstances, with the scurrilous young Uranian author who had penned *The Garden God*. In essence, James was refusing to recognise that, at the very least, his *Turn of the Screw* and his "Pupil" both hint at the same eroticism that he found reprehensible in

Reid's short novel. This led Reid to conclude that James's letter was "prompted by a strange moral timidity, which refuses to accept responsibility for what deliberately has been suggested."[88] As Reid further explains in his second autobiography, *Private Road*: "My admiration for the artist remained, but an admiration more human and intimate had been lost. The intelligence that had seemed so understanding seemed now less understanding."[89]

Although Reid later sent a presentation copy of the first edition of *The Bracknels* to James, complete with an autograph inscription, the arrival of this volume (the copy of which is now in the Forrest Reid Collection at the University of Exeter) was never acknowledged by James, nor were the other presentation copies that Reid sent to him in the coming years. As far as "the Master" was concerned, their acquaintanceship was over, a lesson that Reid subsequently refused to pass on to his own admirers, which may account for his lack of reticence when John Hampson dedicated to him the strikingly homoerotic novel *Saturday Night at the Greyhound* (1931).

On the other hand, perhaps James merely feared that, like Oscar Wilde, Reid was seeking pseudo-martyrdom through his daring, and wished no part of it. While it is true that James's beloved Sturgis had indeed published *Tim*, it should be remembered that he had done so in 1891, years before the Wilde debacle. James undoubtedly recognised that, in 1905, *The Garden God* would be greeted by a post-Wildean audience, an audience that would intuit for itself what Reid would later admit in *Apostate*:

> It is as if we actually could get closer to truth through fiction than through fact. [. . .] I may promise to present it and the people who lived in it without a rag of disguise, but I know I cannot keep my promise.[90]

Perhaps James saw farther than he has been given credit for, especially given that the dedication to him was, after all, a paltry substitute for that suppressed dedication to Andrew Rutherford, complete with its envoy admitting how close "truth" and "fiction" really were for Forrest Reid, "without a rag of disguise":

When you have closed this book, lean back and dream
Of him who made it, and the tender love
He had for you: and how in every word
He wrote of these two boys that love did seem
To be foreshadowed, till at last above
The lonely silence of his life he heard
The god that spoke to bid his dream come true.

Although Reid would, later in life, suggest that this early novel be banished to "the darkest corner reserved for disowned juvenilia,"[91] it nonetheless provides a microcosm of much that appears in his later works. In fact, it forecasts a far more daring project, one that was never actually begun, as Taylor relates:

> Perhaps Forrest Reid's most important book was one which, in the end, he never wrote. This was to be a novel called *The Green Avenue* and was to deal with the theme of pederasty in a more explicit way than he had ever attempted. The earliest mention of the book comes in letters which Reid wrote in 1928. It was to have been a school story; a boy is expelled because of his love for another. [. . .] As the story progresses, it appears that what both parents and schoolmasters are really afraid of is not the suspected—and unproven—sexual contact but the growing realisation that the boy really is deeply in love with his friend.[92]

This more overt version of *The Garden God* promised to be far too daring—hence, far too dangerous—which prompted Marc-André Raffalovich to write to Reid in February 1928, hoping to dampen his zeal for the project: "I should not encourage you to give a year to *The Green Avenue* for fear of grieving all the many who love your former books."[93] In this particular case, as Reid would later explain to Stephen Gilbert, he was actually more concerned that he would "embarrass his friends,"[94] a confession that reveals that there was, and probably ever had been, a tension between "Forrest Reid, the Uranian Author" and "Forrest Reid, the Friend."

Since, in Keatsian fashion, Reid had always placed friendship above all else, *The Green Avenue*, a novel that he had hoped to write for the better part of two decades, remained unwritten, though this masterpiece can be seen in cameo in *The Garden God*, providing yet another reason for why this short novel is vital for a proper understanding and assessment of Forrest Reid, one of the major Uranians.

MICHAEL MATTHEW KAYLOR

Brno

April 4, 2007

ABOUT THE EDITOR

MICHAEL MATTHEW KAYLOR is Assistant Professor of English in the Department of English and American Studies, Faculty of Arts, Masaryk University, Brno, Czech Republic. His principal areas of research are Romantic and Victorian poetry, the British Decadent movement, textual editing, book culture, and Gay Studies. His recently published *Secreted Desires: The Major Uranians: Hopkins, Pater and Wilde* (Brno, Czech Republic: Masaryk University Press, 2006) is the first book-length study on the pederastic Uranians since Timothy d'Arch Smith's *Love in Earnest* (London: Routledge & Kegan Paul, 1970). He is presently working on a biography of Gerard Manley Hopkins and a book on Henry James.

NOTES TO THE INTRODUCTION

1   *The Garden God*, p. 11.

2   Peter Coveney, *Poor Monkey: The Child in Literature* (London: Rockliff, 1957), p. 220.

3   Brian Taylor, *The Green Avenue: The Life and Writings of Forrest Reid, 1875-1947* (Cambridge: Cambridge University Press, 1980), p. 1.

   Only three scholarly books have ever been published about Forrest Reid—Russell Burlingham, *Forrest Reid: A Portrait and a Study* (London: Faber & Faber, 1953); Mary Bryan, *Forrest Reid* (Boston: G. K. Hall, 1976) [in the "Twayne's English Authors Series"]; and Taylor, *Green Avenue*. The present volume is the first scholarly edition of a book by Forrest Reid. Given the limited materials in print, the present volume has relied heavily on the scholarship of Taylor, who himself relied heavily on the scholarship of Burlingham. Only on a single occasion has Bryan's volume been cited.

4   "Pan of Ulster," *Times Literary Supplement* (27 March 1953), p. 204.

5   Forrest Reid, *W. B. Yeats: A Critical Study* (London: Martin Secker, 1915), p. 60.

6   Paul Goldman, "Preface," in *Retrospective Adventures: Forrest Reid: Author and Collector*, ed. by Paul Goldman and Brian Taylor (Aldershot, Hampshire, UK: Scolar Press, with the Ashmolean Museum, Oxford, 1998), p. ix.

7   Christopher Fitz-Simon, "Forrest Reid Remembered," in *Retrospective Adventures: Forrest Reid: Author and Collector*, ed. by Paul Goldman and Brian Taylor (Aldershot, Hampshire, UK: Scolar Press, with the Ashmolean Museum, Oxford, 1998), pp. 5-6 (p. 6).

8   *Garden God*, p. 12.

9   Forrest Reid, *Apostate* (London: Constable, 1926), p. 29.

10   Ibid., p. 203.

11   As quoted in Taylor, *Green*, p. 46.

12   Colin Cruise, "Introduction," in Forrest Reid, *The Garden God* (London: Brilliance Books, 1986), pp. iii-viii (p.v). This (mis)use of the word "homosexual" is also evident throughout Colin Cruise, "Error and Eros: The Fiction of Forrest Reid as a Defence of Homosexuality," in *Sex, Nation, and Dissent in Irish Writing*, ed. with intro. by Éibhear Walshe (New York: St. Martin's, 1997), pp. 60-86.

13   Taylor, *Green*, p. 2. The word "pederasty" derives from *pæderastia*, a Latin word arising from the Greek word *paiderastês* (παιδεραστής)— *pais* (παῖς) "boy" plus *erastês* (ερστής) "lover"—such that "boy-love"

is merely a literal, modernised translation. Since most of the prominent Uranians were Oxford graduates in Classics, they tended to use the term "pederasty," though they employed both terms synonymously, often in the same sentence, as Symonds does in the following: "What the Greeks called *paiderastia*, or boy-love, was a phenomenon of one of the most brilliant periods of human culture"—J. A. Symonds, *A Problem in Greek Ethics: Being an Inquiry into the Phenomenon of Sexual Inversion* (London: Privately printed, [1901]), p. 1. Like Taylor, I have chosen to employ the term "pederasty" rather than more contemporary concepts like "pedophilia" and "ephebophilia" (terms that are often emotive as well as referential).

It must be admitted that, for the Victorians and the Edwardians, there was a rather blurred overlap between "the pederastic" (boy-love) and "the homoerotic" (man-love); and that often their literary and other creations included elements of both, a feature acknowledged by both d'Arch Smith and James Kincaid—see James R. Kincaid, *Child-Loving: The Erotic Child and Victorian Culture* (New York: Routledge, 1992), p. 176. However, what John Pollini notes about Greco-Roman pederasts is equally true for their Victorian and Edwardian counterparts: "What mattered most was not so much the chronological age of an adolescent but how long he was able to maintain his boyish good looks and, most important, a smooth and hairless body and face"—"The Warren Cup: Homoerotic Love and Symposial Rhetoric in Silver," *Art Bulletin*, 81.1 (1999), pp. 21-52 (p. 34). As the Uranian writer Frederick William Rolfe, Baron Corvo (1860-1913) relates about one boy:

> He'll be like this till spring, say 3 months more. Then some great fat slow cow of a girl will just open herself wide, and lie quite still, and drain him dry. First, the rich bloom of him will go. Then he'll get hard and hairy. And, by July, he'll have a moustache, a hairy breast for his present great boyish bosom, brushes in his milky armpits, brooms on his splendid young thighs, and be just the ordinary stevedore to be found by scores on the quays.

—Frederick Rolfe (Baron Corvo), *The Venice Letters*, ed. with intro. by Cecil Woolf (London: Cecil & Amelia Woolf, 1974), p. 37.

This attraction to the qualities of "boyishness" is evident in the following description by Grace, the younger sister of Reid's beloved Kenneth Hamilton, recollecting as an adult: "His love for Kenneth I took wholly for granted, but naturally enough, I suppose, I felt left out. He used to pet the boy, taking him on his knee. I saw nothing out of the way in this either, apart from wondering what anyone could see that was cuddly in a knobble-kneed schoolboy" (as quoted in Taylor, *Green*, p. 100).

14 Ibid., p. 174.

15 Ibid.

16 Lord Alfred Douglas, "Two Loves," in [John Francis Bloxam, ed.,] *The Chameleon: A Bazaar of Dangerous and Smiling Chances*, 1 (December 1894) (London: Gay and Bird)—reprinted in Caspar Wintermans, *Alfred Douglas: A Poet's Life and His Finest Work* (London: Peter Owen, 2007), pp. 210-11.

17 E. M. Forster, *Commonplace Book*, ed. by Philip Gardner (Stanford, CA: Stanford University Press, 1985), pp. 185-86.

18 "People thought it dreadful of me to have entertained at dinner the evil things of life, and to have found pleasure in their company. But they [. . .] were delightfully suggestive and stimulating. It was like feasting with panthers. The danger was half the excitement"—from *De Profundis*, in *The Soul of Man and Prison Writings*, ed. by Isobel Murray (New York: Oxford University Press, 1998), pp. 38-158 (p. 132).

19 See F. B. Smith, "Labouchere's Amendment to the Criminal Law Amendment Bill," *Historical Studies*, 17.67 (1976), pp. 165-73; Nicholas C. Edsall, *Toward Stonewall: Homosexuality and Society in the Modern Western World* (Charlottesville: University of Virginia Press, 2003), pp. 111-14.

20 As quoted in Richard Ellmann, *Oscar Wilde*, rev. edn (New York: Knopf, 1988), p. 409, note.

21 For a discussion of this scandal, see d'Arch Smith, pp. 27-29; H. Montgomery Hyde, *The Cleveland Street Scandal* (New York: W. H. Allen, 1976); Morris Kaplan, "Did 'My Lord Gomorrah' Smile?: Homosexuality, Class and Prostitution in the Cleveland Street Affair," in *Disorder in the Court: Trials and Sexual Conflict at the Turn of the Century*, ed. by George Robb and Nancy Erber (New York: New York University Press, 1999), pp. 78-99.

22 Linda Dowling, *Hellenism and Homosexuality in Victorian Oxford* (Ithaca, NY: Cornell University Press, 1994), p. 114.

23 William Johnson (*later* Cory) (1823-92), who was educated at Eton and King's College, Cambridge, returned to Eton in 1845 as a Classics master, and taught there until dismissed in 1872:

> In April 1872 Johnson suddenly resigned at Eton, and no one can be quite sure of the exact circumstances of his resignation. There is no question, however, that he was dangerously fond of a number of boys. Although he probably did not allow his affec-

tions to take any physical form, he permitted intimacies between
the boys. This conduct was brought to the notice of the head-
master, James Hornsby, who demanded Johnson's resignation,
and Johnson retired quietly.

—Tim Card, "William Johnson Cory," *Oxford Dictionary of National
Biography*, online version (Oxford: Oxford University Press, 2004-
06). See also d'Arch Smith, p. 6. Johnson's influence is evident in the
number of his "favourite" students who became influential Uranians:
Howard Overing Sturgis (1855-1920), Reginald Baliol Brett (1852-1930;
2nd Viscount Esher), Archibald Philip Primrose (1847-1929; 5th Earl of
Rosebery), Oscar Browning (1837-1923), and Digby Mackworth Dol-
ben (1848-67). Johnson also extended his influence through his collection of verses *Ionica* (1858).

24   Walter Horatio Pater (1839-94) was, in many ways, the centre around
which the early Uranian movement revolved. For this reason, a single endnote is insufficient to do him and his influence any justice.
His influence is explored throughout my volume *Secreted Desires*
(2006).

25   John Addington Symonds (1840-93), one of the major homoerotic
and pederastic apologists of the nineteenth century, is almost as
problematic to encompass in an endnote as Pater. The following are
important sources to consider in regard to his role in the Uranian
movement: Joseph Cady, "'What Cannot Be': John Addington Symonds' *Memoirs* and Official Mapping of Victorian Homosexuality,"
Victorian Newsletter, 81 (1992), pp. 47-51; Phyllis Grosskurth, ed. with
intro., *The Memoirs of John Addington Symonds* (New York: Hutch-
inson, 1984); Herbert M. Schueller and Robert L. Peters, eds, *The
Letters of John Addington Symonds*, 3 vols (Detroit, MI: Wayne State
University Press, 1967-69).

26   Oscar Wilde, *The Picture of Dorian Gray*, in *The Complete Works of
Oscar Wilde*, 3rd edn (Glasgow: Harper Collins, 1994), pp. 17-159 (p. 17).

27   William F. Shuter, "The 'Outing' of Walter Pater," *Nineteenth Century
Literature*, 48.4 (1994), pp. 480-506 (p. 506).

28   Edward Carpenter, *My Days and Dreams, Being Autobiographical Notes*,
2nd edn (London: George Allen & Unwin, 1916), p. 196.

29   Walter de la Mare, "Introduction" to Russell Burlingham, *Forrest
Reid: A Portrait and a Study* (London: Faber & Faber, 1953), pp. 9-10 (p.
10). "The original version of this book Reid had called *Youth, Beasts,
Gods, Earth* and the manuscript had contained forty-three poems
not included in the published version. Many of the deletions were
from his translations of Strato, which were 'of a special kind, being

devoted exclusively to poems about boys.' The inclusion—and the subsequent deletion—is both typical and significant" (Taylor, *Green*, pp. 173-74). Norman Vance, "Decadence from Belfast to Byzantium," *New Literary History*, 35.4 (2004), pp. 563-72 (p. 568): "His adroit and effective prose translations from the Greek Anthology, eventually published in 1943, are homage to late classicism and evidence of a kind of Alexandrian decadence, of a determined refusal to connect with a world in which Great Pan is dead."

30 Walter Pater, *The Renaissance: Studies in Art and Poetry*, 4ᵗʰ edn, ed. by Donald L. Hill (Berkeley: University of California Press, 1980 [1893]), p. xxiii.

31 "Pan of Ulster," *TLS*, p. 204.

32 *Uncle Stephen*, in *Tom Barber: Young Tom, The Retreat, Uncle Stephen*, with intro. by E. M. Forster (New York: Pantheon, 1955), pp. 335-572 (p. 442).

33 Reid, *Apostate*, p. 19.

34 Taylor, *Green*, p. 23.

35 Reid, *Apostate*, p. 235.

36 Taylor, *Green*, p. 37.

37 Andrew Rutherford was shown a rough version of the proposed novel *The River*, a novel that found its first appearance in print as the much altered *The Kingdom of Twilight*, the tale of an imaginative boy who returns to his repressive family in Ireland after being expelled from his English boarding school. "The theme of [*The River*], albeit transformed from its realistic setting, became that of *The Garden God* six years later"—or put differently, "*The Garden God* [was] the new and 'quite unrecognizable' version of *The River*" (Taylor, *Green*, pp. 32; 38).

38 As quoted in ibid., p. 37.

39 Ibid., p. 51.

40 Ibid., p. 86.

41 Forster, *Commonplace Book*, p. 102. Osbert Burdett (1885-1936) was a prolific biographer of a flurry of individuals—including William Blake, W. E. Gladstone, the Brownings, and Coventry Patmore—as well as the writer of more general volumes such as his *Beardsley Period* and *Little Book of Cheese* (at which Forster takes a swipe). His eroticism is probably best indicated by the fact that he co-authored, along with E. H. Goddard, *Edward Perry Warren: The Biography of a Connoisseur* (London: Christophers, 1941).

The Savile Club, in Mayfair, London, was and still remains one of the most prestigious private clubs in Britain. By the turn of the century, the Club was at 107 Piccadilly, from whence it moved next door to the Park Lane Hotel, then later to its current location, an eighteenth-century house at 69 Brook Street. The Club was frequented by literary luminaries such as H. G. Wells, Rudyard Kipling, Max Beerbohm, W. B. Yeats, and Thomas Hardy.

42 Taylor, *Green*, p. 175.

43 Ibid., p. 86.

44 Reid, *Yeats*, p. 150. Reid did make "occasional visits" to friends, especially in the last decades of his life. See Burlingham, *Reid*, p. 19.

45 Taylor, *Green*, pp. 91-92.

46 Ibid., p. 101.

47 As quoted in ibid., pp. 101-02.

48 Reid, *Apostate*, p. 21.

49 Burlingham, *Reid*, p. 28.

50 Ibid., pp. 24-25.

51 Norman Vance, "The Necessity of Forrest Reid," in *Retrospective Adventures: Forrest Reid: Author and Collector*, ed. Paul Goldman and Brian Taylor (Aldershot, Hampshire, UK: Scolar Press, with the Ashmolean Museum, Oxford, 1998), pp. 7-9 (p. 7).

52 As quoted in Burlingham, *Reid*, p. 28; Taylor, *Green*, p. 137.

53 Taylor, *Green*, p. 137.

54 As quoted in ibid., p. 105.

55 Stephen Gilbert (b. 1912) was born in Newcastle, County Down, and later became a successful seed merchant, writing novels in his spare time. He is the author of *The Landslide* (1943; dedicated to Reid), *Bombardier* (1944), *Monkeyface* (1948), *The Burnaby Experiments* (1952), and *Ratman's Notebooks* (1968).

About Reid's acquisition of this new infatuation and protégé, Taylor writes: "Reid's friendship with Stephen Gilbert lasted for the next nineteen [*sic*] years; it was not entirely a successful one. Perhaps the fault lay with Reid. Perhaps, after the disappointments of Andrew, then of James Rutherford, and then of Kenneth Hamilton, he thought himself incapable of love and responded too eagerly when friendship came again" (*Green*, p. 138). However, Reid liked to hint, at least to his pederastic friends, that this relationship was more intimate than Platonic, as is evident in a poetic ditty he wrote about an excursion he and Gilbert had made together to Glenagivney (see ibid., p. 149).

After Reid's death, Gilbert provided the following assessment of their relationship: "During all the nineteen [*sic*] years I knew him my feelings for Forrest Reid were mixed. Time and again I wished he would take himself out of my life, that he had never come into it. I felt bitterly that he had stolen my youth. I knew that he had given me a great deal in exchange. I carry these gifts with me yet. And for good or bad he influenced my writing"—Stephen Gilbert, "A Successful Man," *Threshold*, 28 (Spring 1977), p. 106. See Taylor, *Green*, p. 166.

56 Taylor, *Green*, p. 175.

57 Ibid., p. 5.

58 Percy Bysshe Shelley, "Hymn to Pan," in *The Poetical Works of Percy Bysshe Shelley*, ed. by William Michael Rossetti, in 3 vols (London: Gibbings, 1894), III, pp. 66-67 (lines 22-24).

59 Reid, *Apostate*, p. 7.

60 Burlingham, *Reid*, p. 41. Noteworthy here is a passage from Pater's then-infamous "Conclusion" to *The Renaissance* (1893, pp. 187-88):

> Experience, already reduced to a group of impressions, is ringed round for each one of us by that thick wall of personality through which no real voice has ever pierced on its way to us, or from us to that which we can only conjecture to be without. Every one of those impressions is the impression of the individual in his isolation, each mind keeping as a solitary prisoner its own dream of a world.

61 "Pan of Ulster," *TLS*, p. 204.

62 "There is very little of the European and scarcely more of the specifically Ulster in Forrest Reid's writing. Even in his own province, in his own city, Belfast, he himself was little more than a vaguely apprehended 'name'"—Burlingham, *Reid*, p. 13. It should be noted that this appears to have involved a personal choice on Reid's part, for he had indeed, to an extent, "seen the world": "At Cambridge he had used his vacations to travel on the Continent, and among his papers there still exist copious notes—scribbled on the floridly embossed hotel notepaper—of his impressions in the galleries of Berlin, Prague, Wurzburg or Florence" (ibid., p. 33).

63 These words are fabled to have been from the last phrase uttered by Flavius Claudius Julianus, or "Julian the Apostate" (ca. 331-63 CE), the last pagan Emperor of Rome (361-63 CE), who attempted to restore the Roman world to its former self (its self prior to Emperor Constantine's "Christianising"). See Polymnia Athanassiadi, *Julian and Hellenism: An Intellectual Biography* (Oxford: Clarendon Press, 1981); Adrian Murdoch, *The Last Pagan: Julian the Apostate and the Death of the Ancient World* (Stroud, UK: Sutton, 2003). The lines quoted from Swinburne's "Hymn to Proserpine" are from *The Poems of Algernon Charles Swinburne*, 6 vols (London: Harper, 1904), I, pp. 74-81. "Some-

where behind *Apostate* loomed the figure of Julian the Apostate"—
Vance, in *Retrospective*, p. 8.

64 E. M. Forster, *Commonplace Book*, p. 18. Robert Smythe Hichens, famous as the writer of a satire on Wilde, *The Green Carnation* (published anonymously in 1894), sought to explore "the country of Pan"
in works such as *In the Wilderness* (1917). In his short story "The Man
Who Went Too Far" (1904), E. F. Benson decadently explores the
idea of a "cult of Pan."

65 A plethora of shorter works devoted to Pan were produced during
this period, such as two poems published in 1906 by Walter de la
Mare, who would later become a close friend of Forrest Reid. See
"They Told Me"—reprinted in *Poems, 1901 to 1918*, 2 vols (London:
Constable, 1920), I, p. 7; and "Sorcery"—reprinted in ibid., p. 8 (lines
1-5; 26-30).

66 See "Pan's Pupil", pp. 93-96 in the present volume.

67 "Pan of Ulster," *TLS*, p. 204.

68 Walter Pater, *Plato and Platonism: A Series of Lectures*, Library edn
(London: Macmillan, 1920 [1893]), pp. 231-32.

69 Taylor comments that "Reid's pederasty harked back, as did so many
of his qualities, to their Greek ideal; the relationship of pupil and
teacher" (*Green*, p. 174). For a consideration of this Classical dynamic, see K. J. Dover, *Greek Homosexuality* (Cambridge, MA: Harvard
University Press, 1989), p. 91; J. A. Symonds, *Greek Ethics* [1901], p.
13; Henri I. Marrou, *The History of Education in Antiquity*, trans. by
George Lamb (New York: Sheed and Ward, 1956), p. 31.

This blend of pederasty and pedagogy is always evident in
Reid's novels, where "the relationship is [primarily], of course, that
between boy and older man, and Reid returned to an exploration of
that relationship with Brian and Allingham in *The Gentle Lover*, with
Tom and Uncle Stephen, and with the other Brian and Martin Linton
in *Brian Westby*" (Taylor, *Green*, p. 58).

70 Gerald Monsman, "The Platonic Eros of Walter Pater and Oscar
Wilde: 'Love's Reflected Image' in the 1890s," *English Literature in
Transition (1880-1920)*, 45.1 (2002), pp. 26-45 (p. 28).

71 As quoted in Sylvia Townsend Warner, *T. H. White: A Biography* (London: Jonathan Cape, 1967), pp. 277-78. Terence Hanbury White (1906-
64) is best known for his sequence of novels that became *The Once
and Future King* (1958), which retells Sir Thomas Malory's *Le Morte
d'Arthur*.

72 Dowling, *Hellenism*, pp. 115; 137.

73 David J. DeLaura, *Hebrew and Hellene in Victorian England: Newman,
Arnold, and Pater* (Austin: University of Texas Press, 1969), p. 230.

74 Martin Dillon, *God and the Gun: The Church and Irish Terrorism* (New York: Routledge, 1999), p. 175 (see pp. 169-77).

75 Francis King, "A Lifetime of Childhood" [Review of Brian Taylor, *The Green Avenue*], *Times Literary Supplement* (13 February 1981), p. 160.

76 Alan Hollinghurst, "Forrest Reid" [Letter to the Editor], *Times Literary Supplement* (27 February 1981), p. 229.

77 Francis King, "Forrest Reid" [Letter to the Editor], *Times Literary Supplement* (13 March 1981), p. 285.

78 D'Arch Smith, p. 62.

79 "Pan of Ulster," *TLS*, p. 204.

80 Howard Overing Sturgis, *Tim: A Story of School Life* (London: Macmillan, 1891), p. 68.

81 D'Arch Smith, p. 8.

82 Susan E. Gunter and Steven H. Jobe, ed., *Dearly Beloved Friends: Henry James's Letters to Younger Men* (Ann Arbor: University of Michigan Press, 2001), p. 115.

83 Thomas Chatterton, "Elegy, Written at Stanton-Drew," in *The Poetical Works of Thomas Chatterton*, 2 vols (Cambridge: W. P. Grant, 1842), II, p. 484 (line 6).

84 Taylor, *Green*, p. 45.

85 Ibid., p. 43.

86 "'And the Master was not pleased.' The self-mockery of the simple syllables with their reverse Biblical echoes is a portent of the bitterest literary blow of Forrest Reid's career"—Angela Thirlwell, "Child's-Eye View: The Autobiographies of Forrest Reid," in *Retrospective Adventures: Forrest Reid: Author and Collector*, ed. by Paul Goldman and Brian Taylor (Aldershot, Hampshire, UK: Scolar Press, with the Ashmolean Museum, Oxford, 1998), pp. 17-23 (p. 19). See also Arthur Sherbo, "Henry James and Forrest Reid," *Henry James Review*, 13.1 (1992), pp. 82-87.

87 Forster, *Commonplace Book*, p. 18.

88 Reid, *Private Road*, from pp. 69-70.

89 "Reid [...] is being less than truthful, even with himself. The fuss was about the acceptability of the deliberate suggestion of even a Hellenised version of pederastic love. Henry James was after all—well, himself—and the date of *The Garden God* was 1905" (Taylor, *Green*, p. 45).

90 Reid, *Apostate*, p. 5.

91 See Taylor, *Green*, p. 47.

92 Ibid., p. 186.

93 As quoted in ibid., p. 186.

94 As quoted in ibid.

CHRONOLOGY OF FORREST REID

1875   On 24 June, Forrest Reid is born at 20 Mount Charles, Belfast, the youngest child of Robert Reid (d. 1881) and his wife Frances Matilda Reid, *née* Parr.

1881   His family moves to a lesser house, 15 Mount Charles.

1886   He begins to attend Miss Hardy's Prep School, Cliftonpark.

1888   In September, he becomes a pupil at The Royal Belfast Academical Institution (until December 1891).

1893   He takes up his five-year apprenticeship to Henry Musgrave, the head of a firm of tea and sugar merchants with offices in Ann Street, Belfast. A few months later, Andrew Rutherford also becomes an apprentice in this firm.

1896   In February, he shows Andrew Rutherford several intimate passages from his private journal, revealing his affection for him.

1897   He moves with his mother to 25 Malone Avenue, Belfast.

1901   In December, his mother dies, leaving him a small legacy.

1903   He becomes increasingly close to Andrew Rutherford's brothers, the twins James and William.

1904   His first novel, *The Kingdom of Twilight*, is published.

1905   In October, he begins his undergraduate studies at Christ's College, University of Cambridge. In November, his novel *The Garden God* is published.

1907   In the summer, he tours Europe with James Rutherford (repeated in 1908 and 1911).

1908   He graduates from Cambridge. In November, he takes up residence with James Rutherford at 9 South Parade, Belfast.

1911   *The Bracknels: A Family Chronicle* is published, later occasioning his friendships with Walter de la Mare and E. M. Forster.

1912   In October, his novel *Following Darkness* is published.

1914   He moves with James Rutherford to 12 Fitzwilliam Avenue, Belfast.

1916   In the summer, he befriends twelve-year-old Kenneth Hamilton, a boy around whom he weaves his world until

Hamilton, at sixteen, enlists in the Merchant Service. In October, his novel *The Spring Song* is published.

1917   Given James Rutherford's sudden marriage and his own depression because of this, he moves alone to 62 Dublin Road, Belfast.

1919   *A Garden by the Sea: Stories and Sketches* is published (dated 1918).

1920   *Pirates of the Spring* is published (dated 1919).

1924   In July, he moves into his final residence, 13 Ormiston Crescent, at Knock, on the outskirts of Belfast.

1926   His autobiography *Apostate* is published.

1930   Becomes a Fellow of The Royal Society of Literature.

1931   About this time, he befriends ten-year-old Desmond Montgomery. Early in the year, he befriends nineteen-year-old Stephen Gilbert, who will become his literary executor. In October, his novel *Uncle Stephen* is published.

1934   In February, his widely praised novel *Brian Westby* is published. In July, he receives an honorary doctorate from Queen's University, Belfast.

1936   In March, his novel *The Retreat; or, The Machinations of Henry* is published.

1937   *Peter Waring* (a completely rewritten version of *Following Darkness*) is published.

1940   *Private Road*, his second autobiography, is published.

1941   *Retrospective Adventures* is published.

1943   In November, his prose translation *Poems from the Greek Anthology* is published.

1944   In May, his *Young Tom; or, Very Mixed Company*—a novel that will win the James Tait Black Memorial Prize for that year—is published.

1947   On 4 January, he dies at Warrenpoint, on the coast of County Down, and is buried two days later in Dundonald Cemetery, Knock, Belfast. In September, *Denis Bracknel* (a completely rewritten version of *The Bracknels*) is posthumously published.

1955   *Tom Barber*—containing the novels *Young Tom*, *The Retreat*, and *Uncle Stephen*—is published with an introduction by E. M. Forster.

NOTE ON THE TEXTS

The Garden God: A Tale of Two Boys was published in November 1905 by David Nutt of London. The first impression was a quarto-sized volume bound in limp vellum and stamped in gilt, and sold for fifteen shillings. The second impression appeared in April 1906, bound in green boards, and sold for six shillings. A facsimile reprint of the book appeared in 1986, published by Brilliance Books of London. The Valancourt Books edition, the first ever scholarly edition of the novel, follows the text of the first edition verbatim. "Pan's Pupil" first appeared in the journal *Ulad* in May 1905. In 2005, it was reprinted in a limited edition of 50 copies printed by Mr. Callum James of Portsmouth. The present edition follows verbatim the 1905 text.

ACKNOWLEDGEMENTS

The publisher would like to acknowledge gratefully the Estate of Forrest Reid and its agent, Mr. Andrew Hewson of John Johnson Ltd., for permission to republish *The Garden God* and "Pan's Pupil." Grateful thanks are also due to the Hungarian National Gallery, Budapest, for their kind permission to allow reproduction of the painting *Alvó gyermek (Child Sleeping)* by Mihály Kovács (Oil on canvas; 1850) on the front cover.

THE GARDEN GOD

A Tale of Two Boys

'Take this kiss upon the brow!'

EDGAR ALLAN POE

'Yea, to Love himself is pour'd
    This frail song of hope and fear.
Thou art Love, of one accord
    With kind Sleep to bring him near,
    Still-eyed, deep-eyed, ah, how dear!
        Master, Lord,
    In his name implor'd, O hear!'

D. G. ROSSETTI

TO
HENRY JAMES
THIS SLIGHT TOKEN
OF RESPECT
AND ADMIRATION

I

'Y dear Allingham,'[1] he wrote, 'it is very charming of you to think of venturing into this remote corner of the world for no other reason than to renew our friendship, and I must beg of you to let as little time as possible elapse between your promise and its fulfilment. Not only do I consider your idea a delightful one, but also I venture to find it really courageous, since to look me up again, after so many years, must be to take something remarkably like a leap in the dark. Well! at all events I hope—perhaps I should say fear—that you may not discover in me any extraordinary change. Indeed, from this moment I throw myself entirely upon your mercy, plead guilty to all the charges you bring against me in your letter. It is perfectly true that in living here the life of a hermit—a hermit, I hasten to add, with a taste for the philosophy of Epicurus[2] and Anatole France[3]—I have not in the least fulfilled my duties as a good citizen. Doubtless I am not a good citizen. Doubtless, as you so kindly hint, I ought to have married; but I suppose even *you* will admit that it is now too late—too late for me to think of following your excellent example. I cannot, alas! even pretend that I want to follow it, want to forsake my wilderness.[4] Ah, my dear fellow, I am incorrigible, and you need not expect to find in the middle-aged Graham Iddesleigh[5] an any more satisfactory person than him you found so *unsatisfactory* at Oxford. Do you remember all that I used to be in the

old days?—unreasonable, impractical, quite a worthless fellow! Do you ever remember the old days at all? But of course you must, or you would not have desired to renew them. For myself, you know, it is the one great privilege, the one great occupation of my life—I mean remembering. You will scarce be pleased to learn this, I suppose;—that is, unless you are, with increasing years, grown more tolerant of idleness—a weakness which I confess I do not exactly gather from your letter. But you must forgive me for this and countless other faults. Yes— I remember! Sometimes I remember too much!— remember, in other words, what never really *was*; what, alas! only might have been. You see, the dividing line is so apt to shift a little, grow dimmer, as the years pass. . . . And after all, it is only a kind of feline habit that was born in me, and that keeps me, like a cat, quiet in the sun, or before my fire, dreaming, wandering in the endless woods of Persephone. Over those woods a gentle twilight broods, and the soft shady paths wind about, meet and cross one another, and lose themselves again in cool leafy distances.

'Nevertheless, there have been times—moments of dreadful egotism let me call them—when I have told myself, as you so flatteringly tell me, that had I been born the son of a poor man I might have done something in the world, though exactly what, I am as careful as you yourself are to leave undefined. No! I'm afraid all my gifts may be reduced to this single capacity for sitting in the sun—a capacity that is not of immense value to other people, whatever pleasure it may give to myself. I have an idea, however, that had I lived in the days of Plato, he would have employed me to sweep the walks

of the Academe,[6] or mow the grass, or do something of
that kind. Possibly, even to make myself useful by illus-
trating the doctrine of reminiscence, like the boy in the
Meno;[7] or I might have taken care of the books.

'This last, certainly; for I have a sneaking fondness
for the very cobwebs that gather in the corners of a library. Last night I spent two or three delicious hours in
looking over my own volumes, taking down one after
another from the shelf, and slowly turning their leaves.
Many of them, most of them in fact—for my tastes have
not greatly changed—I had loved in my boyhood, and
these were, I confess, the ones I lingered over longest.
And, in a sense, turning their pages again in the light of
this darker-risen day was like holding up a lamp to the
past; and the soft, gentle dust of the dead years fell all
about me, floated in the air I breathed, delicate, sweet,
and sad.

'O wondrous seed of poetry![8] Happy the child into
whose tender soul you have dropped at his birth! May
he keep until his death the innocence and the heart of
a boy, and may the burden of years and the cares of the
world fall lightly upon him! . . .'

He laid down his pen and turned toward the window, while a smile, a little sad, but singularly sweet and
gentle, passed across his face.

After all! . . . Well, he supposed the years *had* fallen
lightly upon him. If he took the trouble to look
in the glass he must see that his hair was turning
grey, that his shoulders were a little stooped,
that there were lines about his mouth and
eyes. . . . And his life?—that too, perhaps, had taken a

greyish tinge. . . . Monotonous? . . . ah yes, monotonous
in truth: but even now he had only to close his eyes to
bring up the light—the light. . . .

The view of the years that opened up behind him
was in fact tranquil and pleasant enough; uneventful;
like a broad, shady garden, an old-world, sleepy garden
full of flowers still sweet and fresh. He had done little. As
Allingham had pointed out (with something of the air of
a man who has made a wonderful discovery), the years
of his life had simply floated away from him—floated
away just as in autumn dead leaves float down a river.

But there had been many things that had given him
pleasure. On the whole he had been happy—happy after
his fashion: and he had known, had felt, the most beautiful thing of all, 'the ecstasy and sorrow of love. . . . '⁹

He looked out into the quiet evening. The garden
lay before him, stretching from the window in the pale
half-light. A fine misty rain had begun to fall and was
slowly shutting out the world. Presently his gaze wandered back again to the room wherein he sat. It rested
on dark oak carvings; on the sheen and sombreness of
fine bindings; on a chipped and broken statue of a boy,
in yellowish marble; and, lastly, on a modern portrait
hanging above the great fireplace.

This was the only picture in the room, and the fading light had drawn most of the colour out of it, but
his memory held up a lamp—a lamp of soft flame—by
which he beheld the full length figure of a boy—a boy
of fifteen, sixteen, slight, dark-complexioned, with delicately oval face, and long silky hair falling in a single
great wave over his forehead. The features were very

finely moulded; the mouth especially being quite perfect. A somewhat exotic looking youngster, extraordinarily aristocratic one imagined, even a little disdainful,—yes, that too, perhaps, despite the wonderful charm of expression.

Harold, youngest son of Aubrey Stewart Brocklehurst, Esquire.[10] He remembered the name as he had seen it in a catalogue of the Royal Academy[11]—how long ago? He remembered the strange conversation he had had later on with his father, when he must have laid bare his soul a little; he remembered the morning when, on coming downstairs, he had found the picture there, awaiting him.

Twenty—thirty years ago!—it seemed like yesterday. Surely his father had been very good to him! The picture, from what he had since heard of the character of Mr. Brocklehurst, had not been bought for nothing. . . . And Harold! . . .

Thus he had been when he had first met him; thus he was now; thus he would be for ever! For he would never grow old—he would be a boy always. Summer would follow summer and the fields would grow white to harvest, but Time would thread no silver in the dusk of his dark hair, nor dim his smile, nor make unshapely his shapely body.

Graham lay back in his chair and closed his eyes. He had already forgotten his unfinished letter to Allingham; he had forgotten everything—everything save the curious fantastic dream that had filled up the first part of his life—the great light—the light beyond. . . .

How had it begun? . . . Had it always been? . . . He tried to remember. . . .

Presently he made a movement to light a cigar. Nothing now was visible in the room save, very faintly, the broken statue, an antique version of the famous Spinario,[12] which his father had come by, he knew not how, long ago, in one of his many wanderings through Greece. And it came suddenly into Graham's mind that this statue was the centre from which everything had radiated; the touchstone around which his whole life had revolved. *It* was the beginning, then—the starting point. And yet—had it only begun with his life here? Had it not been before? . . . Two thousand years ago? . . . But the veil had descended—he could not see.

This Greek boy, at all events, had been his secret playmate throughout his childhood, the companion who had shared his numerous adventures, the companion of his dreams—day-dreams and sleeping-dreams. And his mind leapt back to the dawn of his life. He had been brought up by his father (his mother had died in giving him birth), brought up here, in this house; and until he had gone to school he had had no friend of his own age. His father had himself undertaken his education, had taught him to read Greek at an age when most boys are stumbling through the first page of their grammar, and before Graham had ever heard of either Shakespeare or Milton, he had read again and again many of the writings of Sophocles and Plato.

Given such influences—his unconventional upbringing, his ignorance of the world, his beautiful surroundings—was it a wonder that that strange faculty for dreaming with which he had been born should have been perfected—perfected until in broad daylight he would slip unconsciously from one world to the other, and gravely tell his father of marvellous happenings, fantastic adventures, which never could have taken place? Yes, there had been magic influences at work in that sleepy garden, in those broad, soft lawns and quiet trees,—a magic, above all, in the dim rich music of the sea.

For through all his childhood a subtle music had whispered like an undersong[13]—the music of water, the music of running water, of sighing water—seeming to shape his very soul, making it pliant, graceful, gentle and pure, giving to it that gift or malady of reverie, which was itself like the endless flowing away of a stream. The noise of water had been ever in his ears. At night, if he had chanced to awaken, he had heard the low sad wash of the waves; in the daytime he had often lain for hours on the bank of a stream that flowed among the roots of water-willows by the foot of the apple-orchard,—lain there and let his thoughts run on and on with the running water, so fresh! so clear! so pure! And in the rose-garden there was an old moss-stained fountain, a fountain that sang in the sunshine, and wept in the twilight, and sobbed in the night—a fountain that murmured through the noontide to a lazy boy, whispering of the wanderings of Odysseus, and of Jason and the golden fleece—a fountain that curved up against the blue and splashed back into a basin of broad green leaves—a fountain coloured by the rainbow of romance, and brushed by the outstretched wings of Love.

Sometimes in the evenings he would sit for a while with his father on the lawn before the house, or play a game of croquet with him; and sometimes in the mornings he did his lessons there, or in the side-garden, while the scent of roses, and the low booming whisper of the bees, drifted slowly past. And whenever he looked up he would see, stretching away from him, trim dark walks, and soft green turf, and brilliant flower-beds, all very still and quiet under a yellow summer sun—he would see arches of climbing roses, dahlias with their petals opened wide to the heat, the sunlight itself, like a stream of daffodils, falling from the deep blue sky. A place to dream the sleepy hours away! a place suggestive of, leading to, that inner contemplative life, to the boy, even then, so precious! And looking at it now, in retrospect, he was conscious of a drowsy calm that had hung everywhere and over everything, hardly stirring with the faint wind; an absolute freedom from all troublous things, from all the tumult and discord of the world. Attuned to such surroundings he had grown up; on hot afternoons lying in the dark, cool, fragrant shadow of a great beech tree that grew close to the house—not reading, feeling rather than thinking, letting the impression of everything about him sink into his soul, to be afterwards an ever-present picture there, a picture of perfect beauty, of that ideal or spiritual beauty which, according to Plato, must lift one's spirit to God—willing to live and die just there, never wandering quite so far afield even, as those dark blue hills one could see, from the upper windows, melting into the sky.

A rather sensuous boy perhaps![14] One, certainly, for whom the actual colour, the physical charm of life, of the visible world, meant much. A gentle boy too; warm-hearted, loving and happy, innocent and pure. . . .

The visible world!—was it not almost sentient? From the trees and the sky, from the restless sea and the wind had emerged, at any rate, that imaginary playmate who had made his life beautiful; the messenger of Eros; the fair boy who had come to him from his strange garden, his meadow of asphodel.[15]

And then—he had gone to school.

II

 HEY had indeed often discussed it. It had been perpetually there—a source of wonder and many questions—a thing which hovered and danced, drew near and retreated, a thing which could be referred to at any moment without notice or introduction, a kind of enchanted castle which grew up into the sky with lightning-like rapidity, and as quickly vanished. It had not been, however, until he was close on sixteen[16] that the decisive step had been actually taken, that the vision had given place to reality.

His father brought him and departed again, leaving Graham with a sinking heart in the midst of his new world. How dreadfully different from anything he had ever known it was all going to be! For the first time in his life he felt thoroughly miserable.

Yet, in a way, he was to be singularly fortunate. Far sooner than might have been expected he dropped into his new life. He had never, of course, played either cricket or football, but he was naturally strong and agile, and in the former game he now made rapid progress. It was then that he learned how ready his new companions were with their praise and encouragement. If he had known more of the world, indeed, he might have marvelled not a little at his almost immediate popularity, for doubtless, at first, he could not but have seemed 'rather queer' to the others. Nevertheless they liked him, liked to be with him, and if they occasionally found him alarmingly innocent—well! somehow, it was only charming that he should be so. To be sure he *was*, now and again, made fun of in a way; but that way was quite the kindliest in the world, the very opposite from the way they might have taken had they been so minded, had their desire been to hurt, to torment him.

All this, however, the fact that his new friends had so at once and unreservedly welcomed him, had made it so tremendously easy for him, seemed to Graham to be merely natural, and thus, in a sense, it probably defeated his father's main object in sending him to school at all; that object being, presumably, to familiarise him with the ways of actual life. From Graham, somehow, actual life was as far away as ever. It was all so bright, so charming; every one was so 'decent' to him, so nice; how in the world was he to know that 'niceness' wasn't a thing to be counted upon; and that he, Graham Iddesleigh, wonderfully had been made an exception of? There seemed in fact to be hardly a boy who was not anxious to help him, who did not take a pleasure in watching him drop into the ways of the place; while such things as he really did do well—swimming, diving, running, leaping, translating Greek—were elaborately overpraised. The masters liked him also; and, what was more significant, the older boys, who ignored his contemporaries, took an interest in him, asked him to their studies, looked after him, wanted him to do the school credit.

He was happy. The days passed very quickly. Nevertheless, he had not quite learned to live the life the others lived, and there were times when he felt homesick. One thing in particular he noticed (though he had made too many new friends to find much leisure for regret), and that was just that the old playmate of his dreams had ceased to visit him, that he could no longer even call up very clearly his image, remember what he was like.[17] It was as if the change which had come into his everyday world had extended on into the dusky ways of sleep, and though he did not dwell upon it at all, yet he felt, obscurely, that something that had been had ceased to be, and that there was a blank, a void in his existence, which none of the many new pleasures and interests in his life would ever be able to fill.

III

O N a fallen stone, under the shelter of a rough, loosely-piled wall, Graham sat. All around him the landscape stretched, field after field, bleak and bare in the cold wintry light of a February afternoon, while dark heavy clouds blew like puffs of smoke across the dull grey sky. From time to time a passing breath of wind shivered through the dry grass, and from time to time a pale yellowish light, like a dim reflection of some wan remote sunshine, washed through the clouds, brightening the country for a few moments. The boy's chin was supported between his hands, and he gazed out across the monotonous fields and naked hedges, listlessly, a little sadly, thinking of home, of the past. He felt tired; there was a dampness, a heaviness, in the air, which weighed upon his spirit; and something of his dejection was visible in the mere drooping of his head.

He had passed from the golden quiet of his home into the midst of a large public school, into a busier, noisier world, where the real and the ideal no longer melted into a single dreamy haze; and when he looked back across the narrow stream of time—those few intervening weeks!—he could not but marvel at its depth. His former life had fallen from him like the sinking of a picture in the fire, and he knew that it would never come again. It was over! . . . finished! . . . done with! . . . How strange! . . . Yet when he closed his eyes it unrolled itself like a broad scroll, clear in every detail. . . . Then, when the voice of water, and the whisper of the wind in the trees and in the grass had been for him almost as the sound of human voices, and the broad open sky and sea as the sight of human faces—then, when such things had seemed to have the power to speak to him directly, to speak from their own soul to his—when Pan and his followers had been in every thicket by the way![18] Ah! gazing back upon it all from his present position, he found time to wonder—to wonder gravely, doubtfully— if that clear, pure atmosphere would ever again droop its wings above him, if things would ever be again, even for a little, as before. Those long, peaceful summer days, and cool, lingering evenings, when he had sat upon the steps beside his father, watching him smoke his pipe, and chattering to him of the different ideas and plans that danced, or lingered in his mind, while the trees seemed to rest so softly in the quiet air, so softly against the sky! . . . A sudden wild longing for it all, for all his old life, arose within him, and in a passion of homesickness he flung himself down in the swaying, sapless grass, and seemed to hear the moaning of a sea that was break- ing, miles and miles away, upon a curved rocky shore, to hear the harsh screams of the sea-gulls as they flew restlessly over the grey bare waste of water, and dipped to the tumbling waves.

All at once he was aroused by a foot-fall, a rustle in the grass, and still half-blinded by his dream, turned to face the intruder.

'What is the matter? Can I help you at all?'

The words were very gently spoken, and came to Graham with a curious familiarity and charm. But in- stead of answering he sat quite still, gazing fixedly at the stranger, his colour gradually deepening. Fascinated, spell-bound, his lips parted, his eyes opened wide, he hardly dared to move lest the vision should vanish. For some moments indeed he scarce drew his breath; for some moments it seemed as though his whole vital force were concentrated into one long steadfast gaze.

He who stood before him, nevertheless, was but a boy of about his own age and height, though more slightly built. For Graham, however, he was beautiful as an angel—was, in truth, a kind of angel, a 'son of the morning.'[19] His skin—contrasting with the broad linen collar he wore—was of that dark, olive-brown hue which the Greeks, in their own boys, believed to be indicative of courage;[20] his eyes were blue and dark and clear, his nose straight, his mouth extraordinarily fine, delicate; his dark hair, soft and silky, falling in a single great wave over his shapely forehead.

'Who are you?' Graham faltered.

The boy began to blush a little—then to smile. 'My name is Brocklehurst—Harold Brocklehurst. . . . Why do you look at me so strangely?'

His question made Graham suddenly conscious of his rudeness, and also of the childishness, the impossibility of the idea that had floated into his mind. 'I did not mean to,' he stammered, covered with confusion. 'I beg your pardon.' Then, with his eyes lowered: 'You remind me very much of some one I know. . . . It is rather queer . . . and . . . and you took me by surprise. . . . I was so unprepared.'

'Unprepared!'

'Yes. . . . I was thinking of him—of the other—when you came up. . . . You don't understand, of course. It is the extraordinary likeness—and it *is* extraordinary'—he could not help looking at the boy again.

'But likeness to whom?' Brocklehurst wondered. 'And why should it startle you?'

'Ah, to whom?' Graham echoed enigmatically. His strange fancy still hung there in the air before him, hung about his interlocutor like a light, like a blaze of dazzling sunlight. 'I don't know,' he softly added.

'You don't know!' Brocklehurst paused, just a little taken aback. Then as he noticed the other's seriousness he began to laugh. 'Aren't you a rather queer fellow?' he suggested with a kind of charming easiness.

'We are both a little queer,' Graham answered. 'At least . . . I beg your pardon——'

'Oh, it's all right.'

'You see—you see I have known you for so long that—that—— ' His explanation, whatever it might have been, died away.

'You mean you have *really* known me. Then you must have met me somewhere before to-day!' He tried to recall the occasion, but without success.

'It was not here,' Graham went on slowly, gravely. 'I—I can't tell you.' He looked with a wistful, questioning helplessness into his companion's face. 'If I were to tell you, should you laugh?'

'I don't know. At any rate you *want* to tell me?'

'Yes, I want to.'

'Well, fire away then.'

'It is something that is rather hard for me to say. . . . It will make you think me so childish, so silly. . . . You see you couldn't very well believe it unless—unless you yourself were to remember, just as I do—unless it were true——'

Brocklehurst glanced at him quickly. 'Remember having seen *you* somewhere? But I may easily have forgotten. As a matter of fact I have forgotten—so now.'

'Yes—so now. . . . But I know you, for all that—the sound of your voice even, the way you speak and stand there.'

'I only came back this morning. I do not think you were here before Christmas.'

Graham shook his head. 'It was not here,' he murmured. Then suddenly gathering courage, and with his eyes half closed: 'It was far away . . . in a garden . . . Oh, I can't tell you . . . I can't, unless you help me. . . . It slips from me so quickly. . . . When I try to reach it, it fades from me, though I know it is still there . . . there, somewhere'—he smiled a little timidly. 'Do you wonder what I am talking about? . . . I am only trying to remember a dream—a dream I have had so often.'

'And *I* have something to do with it?'

'Oh yes; everything'—he spoke quietly, simply. 'You were always there, you know. It belongs to you as much as it belongs to me. You have been meeting me there for years!'

There was that in his voice which made Brocklehurst, with exquisite tact, look carefully away from him. 'I don't quite follow you,' he said softly. 'I don't think I quite know what you mean.'

'My meaning is only that,' Graham replied; 'only what I have just told you.' He paused as if trying to make it out more clearly for himself. 'Don't *you* sometimes dream?' he asked.

'Yes, of course.'

'Well! has it never seemed to you that there must be another world than this we are living in now?—a world outside this, I mean, but still a real world?'

'A dreamland?'[21]

'Call it what you like. Yes—a dreamland. But while we are there, you know, *it* is the real world, there is no other.'

Brocklehurst looked at him curiously. 'But you don't believe that, do you?'

'Yes, I believe it—or I used to believe it. There is something about it in the *Theœtetus* of Plato.'

'You have read Plato?'

'Only a little. I used to read him with my father.'

'And that is where you got your idea?'

'Oh no; I have always had it. It has been like a part of my life. . . . You see my dreams are rather peculiar . . . I go back in them always to the same place—this garden—and I carry the memory of one life with me into the other. . . . Do you understand now? I can't put it any plainer, because I am a little confused myself. Some day it may become clearer, and I may be able to tell you better.'

'Well!—till then——' and Brocklehurst drew himself up on to the wall and drummed with his heels against the stones.

'Till then?'

'Do you talk in this way to every one?'

'You mean I had better not? How should I talk to other people, when even you do not understand me?'

The other boy was silent. He was thinking. 'What was I like?' he asked presently—'in your dreams, I mean?' Then quickly, and before his companion could reply, 'No; you need not tell me.'

'You do not care for me to talk to you in this way?' Graham questioned half sadly, and with a strange feeling of loneliness creeping over him. 'You were beautiful,' he whispered under his breath; 'more beautiful than any one I have ever seen.'

A long silence followed. If Brocklehurst were surprised by his new friend's last words, he at least showed nothing. The wind stirred faintly above their heads, and a flock of rooks flew homeward across the grey sky. It was already getting late. The world seemed to have floated into a clinging frosty haze, through which a golden moon gleamed, rising slowly up above the bare, desolate fields.

'We had better be going back,' Brocklehurst said. 'It is getting dark.'

They walked slowly toward the school through the gathering dusk. To feel his companion close beside him, and to be alone with him like this, gave Graham an exquisite pleasure. If only he could be brave enough to put his hand upon his shoulder![22] All the way home he kept telling himself he would do so when they reached such and such a point in the road; but each time a curious shyness deterred him, each time his courage failed him; and when they at last reached the school, and his opportunity was gone, he felt as if he had allowed something precious and unrecoverable to slip away for ever.[23]

IV

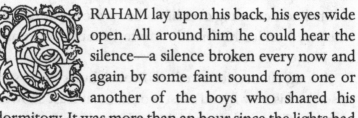RAHAM lay upon his back, his eyes wide open. All around him he could hear the silence—a silence broken every now and again by some faint sound from one or another of the boys who shared his dormitory. It was more than an hour since the lights had been put out, and all save himself were fast asleep; but he lay awake still, thinking of the afternoon that had just passed, and of the strange emotion it had swept into his life. He wondered how it could have come about, and he pondered old tales he had read—some of them long ago—tales of a pagan world, in which this wonderful passion of friendship, then so common, had played its part.[24] Returning to him now, they wore a new and added beauty, a meaning he had only dreamed before, but which at present filled his mind with a kind of heavenly radiance. Might not his own friendship be just the same? . . . Might not it, too, be something more than a mere romantic reverie, than the shadow of a beautiful dream? He felt an exquisite happiness in giving way to his tenderness, in letting his imagination run on and on, like a swift, strong river, in an ever-changing dream of love. It was as if by merely stretching out his hand he had touched the poetry, the soul of existence; it was as if by stretching out his hand he had awakened another spirit to beat its wings within his own.[25]

'Spirit of Beauty, that dost consecrate
With thine own hues all thou dost shine upon.'[26]

So he might have sung had he known the lines. For he felt himself raised up as on the strong, swift wings of the morning, lifted to the very gate of Heaven. It was on such a love as this that the Platonic philosophy had been built;[27] and now—now in his own life—it had come true. Fair, and pure, and holy—down from the garden of God—it had fallen into his soul, had poured through the open gates of Heaven, to bathe him in its light. He turned upon his pillow and smiled. He stretched out his arms wide to the great, fragrant mother-night, and she bent down over him, cool and dark and silent, and kissed him softly on his forehead, and on his mouth and eyes.

He could not sleep. A strange restlessness, a 'spirit in his feet,'[28] seemed to draw him from his bed, and leaving his cubicle, he stood in his night-dress on the cold floor. A flood of moonlight lay across the room, and he watched it falling through the air, a silent, rapid stream.

How still everything was! how light! Softly, softly, on tip-toe, he made his way to the window, and climbing on to a chair, looked out.

In the grounds it was light with that same cold light, clear, yet not quite clear, earth and sky seeming to be blended in one strange misty radiance, pale, bluish, almost white. And the moonlight lay, still and dreamy, everywhere, more tangible, yet more shadowy, than the light of day. If one stretched out one's hands, one might almost feel it, he thought, might almost brush it away like a great white silky cobweb of woven flame. The stone gable of the house stood out sharply black against the sky, and the shadows on the grass were black as ink. Above the long row of still and leafless trees he saw the belt of Orion, and to the right of that, the white, broken

moon faintly edged with blue. It was like the dawning
of some wonderful, icy day upon an unexplored, a new
and mysterious world; and through the cold misty light
he half expected to see the moving forms of those who
live in the unknown.

He did indeed see a figure—a figure coming toward him, stepping slowly down a wide silver stair that
reached from Heaven—a figure clad in fair armour, and
with dark hair floating out against the stars. . . . He was
calling to him from without . . . he beckoned with his
hands . . . he waited, waited. . . .

A shudder ran through Graham's body: he seemed
no longer to be in the dormitory, but to stand somewhere beyond the gates of death. He clasped the bars of
the window with his hands; he leaned against the iron
bars; then he opened out his arms wide and smiled. . . .

'What are you doing? . . . Iddesleigh! . . . Graham!' It
was Brocklehurst's voice. His cubicle was next the window, and he had been awakened.

'Nothing; nothing,' Graham answered, startled, turning quickly round. 'I was looking out. . . . I
forgot. . . . Why are you not asleep?' He went over to
his friend, and sat down by his side. Brocklehurst had
already cuddled under the clothes again.

'I was asleep until you wakened me. Why are you
not in your bed?' he whispered. 'Why were you standing
there? What a mad thing to do at this time of year! You
might kill yourself!'

'Oh, I don't take cold easily. I suppose I wasn't thinking of what I was doing.'

'But you should have put on your dressing-gown.
You are only in your night-dress. At first I thought you

were walking in your sleep. You looked like a white ghost there at the window. You will catch your death of cold now if you stay there. Come in here beside me if you want to talk.'

Graham got into the bed. 'I was thinking of you,' he said softly.

'You're a very strange fellow—aren't you?' Brocklehurst murmured.

'Yes; I suppose so.'

'Hush! Speak lower. If you were caught here with me, you know, there'd be the most frightful row. . . .²⁹ What were you looking at out of the window?'

'I don't know. . . . I seemed to see——'

'What?'

'I can't tell you. I almost forget.'

'You *must* tell me.'

'It was a knight . . . a young knight in armour.'

'Out there on the grass?'

'It was you. . . . Oh, I know there wasn't really anything there,' he added hastily—'only the light of the moon on the ground.'

'And all that you told me this afternoon—it, too, was nothing?'

'Yes—yes, it was. Some day I will tell you all about it, from the very beginning, but not now. It would take too long. . . . You see I was so much by myself before I came here. I had no one. And—and—I could not help speaking to you this afternoon. . . . You don't understand how—how much it is all a part of my life—how much it means to me——' He broke off abruptly, and for a little Brocklehurst said nothing.

'Tell me about what you used to do at home, if you

don't mind,' he whispered presently. Then he lay still, listening to a rather broken and wandering story, which very soon he grew too sleepy to follow. 'You had better go back to your own bed now,' he murmured drowsily. 'It wouldn't do for you to drop off asleep here. Don't make any noise: some other chap may be awake.'

Graham rose obediently, but he still lingered in the cubicle, held by a vague yet very strong desire—desire to unburden himself of that which filled his soul, and which a feeling of shyness kept locked up in his breast. Then suddenly he overcame his cowardice, and kneeling down on the floor beside the bed, he kissed his friend as he lay there half asleep. That was all: he could not have spoken if he had tried to: even as it was his eyes were wet with tears. But he felt a kind of ecstasy of happiness as he stole back to his own bed, for it seemed to him that just then, when his lips had touched Harold's cheek, he had given himself to him for better or worse, had given him his life, his trust. In the morning, he knew, all would be a little different; in the morning he should have to come back to an everyday world. But he should be no longer alone there; oh, he should never be alone again. With his face buried in his pillow, and his cheek still a little damp, he prayed that all might be well, prayed that Harold might come to care for him; and day was breaking when at last he fell asleep.

V

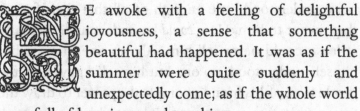E awoke with a feeling of delightful joyousness, a sense that something beautiful had happened. It was as if the summer were quite suddenly and unexpectedly come; as if the whole world were full of happiness and sunshine.

Then he remembered—remembered it all; and a strange passionate tenderness filled his heart. Yes! it *was* the summer—summer indeed—the sun shone all around him. At the same time he felt within him a deep and unaccountable shyness, which kept him from joining his friend, which kept him alone with his own thoughts until morning school was finished.

By then he had turned things over in his mind, by then he had come even to wonder a little at his first be-wilderment. It all seemed now so natural, so only what he had awaited, had come here for. Already a thing without beginning, without end! It was simply there—there like the air he breathed—something that had wrapped itself about his life, his whole being. And it slid back and back, without a break, without a pause, back into the past. There had been no first meeting at all; he had no need even to ask a question; there was no ambiguity to be explained, still less an anomaly. He knew, he felt; and as day followed day, and week followed week, he knew and felt more and more. He listened to the undertone, listened to it growing deeper and more melodious, be-coming at times almost articulate, pointing the way;

only when he strained his ear for the word, the word at last, definite, decisive, it died back again into silence.

And yet he had had other moments—moments when he had seen, or had seemed to see, that Brockle-hurst understood little enough of all that their friend-ship meant to him. How *could* he understand? Graham, at least, could never tell him. Ah, no one, no one but himself understood, no one but himself knew how the gentle tone of his friend's voice had a power to draw the tears to his eyes, a power to sink into his inmost soul. Oh, he loved him so dearly! There was something in the very secrecy of his affection that permitted him to keep it passionately apart from everything else, from his life of everyday, from any vulgar or prosaic encroachment. He kept it in a place sacred, beautiful, quiet; a chapel within his own spirit, a chapel into whose soft light he passed from time to time to worship, to be alone there, alone there with his love, alone there before the altar he had decked with candles and flowers, with the white stainless flowers of his boyish admiration, his innocence and faith. . . .

Nevertheless, little by little, it was forced upon him—incredulous at first, reluctant to believe—that Brockle-hurst's reputation was not a good one. Nothing very precise as yet; only a few vague rumours; but he knew, could easily see, that his friend was not liked. At first he had found this hard to credit, inconceivable almost; but when one boy after another practically advised him to drop his chum he could no longer close his eyes to the fact. Naturally he felt tremendously angry. It seemed so mean, so cowardly, so unfair; for no one, though all were willing enough to hint, to suggest, appeared able to tell

him anything definite. He knew, of course, that Brocklehurst had been absent from the school for a while—had
been removed, more than one boy quite plainly told
him—but even were this the case (and Brocklehurst
himself had never alluded to it), the fact of his having
been brought back again, in Graham's opinion, openly,
triumphantly, established his innocence. And innocence
of what? When all was said and done, one could be sent
away for merely asserting what one believed to be one's
rights—for impatience of routine, a hundred things that
did not in the least imply any serious fault. It must be
confessed that in his heart of hearts he now and then
wondered if assertion of his rights, any more than impatience of routine, could very greatly imperil a boy's
popularity; but it was not until some time had elapsed
that it actually occurred to him that he ought, after all,
to speak to Brocklehurst himself of the matter, not telling him of course how far public opinion was against
him, but putting him a little on his guard, giving him a
little advice.

It was on a Sunday afternoon when they were out
walking together—one of the latter days of spring—
that he finally made up his mind to adopt this line of
conduct; and he approached the subject at once, though
at first a little hesitatingly, and in a rather roundabout
fashion.

'What are you going to be, Harold, when you grow
up,' he asked—'when you leave school and college, I
mean?'

Brocklehurst looked somewhat surprised. 'Be!' he
echoed. 'Oh, I can't tell you that. I haven't even thought
about it yet. . . . Besides I don't want to be anything in

particular. I shall be myself, I suppose—just what I have always been.'

'But I mean what shall you do?' Graham persisted. 'You'll do *something*, of course. What do you think about when you are all alone?'

Brocklehurst smiled. 'Very often of you,'[30] he said lightly. 'Oh, I dare say I shall manage to drift along somehow or other. That is what I do now, you know.'

'Drift?'

'Yes. Don't you think it rather charming?' He spoke in the half-lazy, half-ironic fashion Graham had now grown accustomed to, but which he had noticed to have a curiously irritating effect upon other people. It was indeed just one of the innocent causes of Brocklehurst's unpopularity that he had thought of alluding to, especially since it, more than anything else, tended to make his masters dislike him.

'I haven't any very strong hold upon things,' Brocklehurst amplified. 'Everything seems nice enough until I actually do it; but immediately afterwards it begins to bore me a little. As soon as you've tried a thing, you know, it's apt to become the least bit tiresome. That is why I shouldn't care to tie myself down to anything in particular.'

'But you must, for all that, follow some definite way of life,' Graham answered, dissatisfied.

'My dear fellow, I only want to follow you.'

'Me?'

'Yes, you. I'm not joking at all. Since I've known you a great deal has changed. You've made me see things in a different way. It's perhaps rather extraordinary, but it's true. You're so—what shall I call it?—good.'

'But you don't see them in *my* way,' Graham objected.

'I know—I know. I dare say not even in a way you'd care for. But still there is a great difference from the old way. Only I can't exactly tell you what it is, nor how long it will last. Probably just as long as our friendship. That is why I want to keep close to you. I've been friends with other boys than you, you see,—even with some of those who try now to make you drop me. Look at those two rows of trees, Graham, running side by side for a little, and then suddenly branching off in opposite directions.'

'Well?'

'Well: they are like our destinies.'

Graham glanced at him. 'Why do you say that?' he asked a little strangely.

Brocklehurst smiled. 'That is, if our friendship is ever to be broken,' he explained.

'A real friendship can never be broken,' answered Graham slowly. 'If you think that ours can, then it is not a very great one—even now.'

Brocklehurst nodded his head. 'I wonder what you call a real friendship!'

'Oh, if you have to ask——!'

'It is only because I want you to tell me,' he said softly.

Graham smiled. Then suddenly he saw the opening for which he had been waiting. 'One of the signs of a real friendship is not to be afraid to speak openly to your friend of all that concerns both him and you.'

'Ah, that means you have something rather unpleasant to tell me, doesn't it?' Brocklehurst inquired with a not unkindly irony. 'Friends should have no secrets from each other, I expect?'

'They ought to share everything,' Graham replied simply; 'and more than anything else they ought to share their thoughts.'

Brocklehurst paused. 'Shall we sit down here,' he asked, with a faint sigh, 'before we begin?'

'You make it very hard for me,' Graham murmured, colouring a little.

'Ah, you mustn't mind that.'

They seated themselves on the trunk of a fallen tree, and a rather awkward silence followed.

Below them the ground sloped down, forming a little glen of trees and brambles, through which a narrow stream ran. The sunlight threading its way between the branches turned the raindrops upon the mossy grass to tiny globes of fire; and everywhere there was the fresh, life-giving smell of spring, of earth and moist vegetation. Brocklehurst sat with his chin between his hands; and his face, absolutely immobile, might have been carved in bronze. The corners of his mouth were drooped; and a deep line was drawn down his forehead between his eyes; his eyes, almost black in colour, gazed out straight before him. He appeared to be completely oblivious to Graham's presence, to everything save his own thoughts, and the latter began to wonder a little as to what was passing in his mind.

And as he wondered a new world seemed to dawn upon his consciousness—a world where good and evil no longer stood so very far apart, were no longer so fixedly opposed to each other, so indissoluble as they had been, but were, rather, bound up together, inexplicably and hopelessly, almost defying disentanglement.[31] A moment ago everything had been so clear, so plain before him; now, when he looked up, the sun was a little clouded over, and the whole colour and meaning of life stained with a darker hue. It seemed to him that he had been living in an atmosphere of dreamy idealism, the fruit of a plentiful lack of knowledge; and it did not occur to him that his ignorance had been beautiful, springing, as it did, not from stupidity, but from a peculiar type of mind, and an inexperience of life, of evil, even of sorrow. And a great compassion for the boy beside him welled up in his heart.

'Do you think I tell you everything, then?' Brocklehurst asked suddenly, a half-mocking smile hovering at the corners of his mouth, but in his voice just the faintest tremor.

Graham kept his eyes carefully averted from him. 'I think you would like to,' he answered slowly.

Brocklehurst shook his head. 'No; I shouldn't like to.'

'Well then, you—you can't trust me very much.'

'Ah, but I do trust you. . . . Why do you want to be so serious?' He smiled faintly. 'I notice that you keep all your seriousness for me, who am nevertheless supposed to be your chum.'

Graham looked doubtfully at him. 'Tell me that everything is all right,' he said, 'and I will believe you.'

'Everything is all right.'

There was a silence.

'Do you think you are keeping your promise?' Brocklehurst asked, with a little laugh.

'No; I suppose not.'

'What do you want to hear? What do you want me to tell you? It is foolish, isn't it, to bother about what is horrid, when there is so much that isn't?'

'In you, do you mean?'

'In me, if you like.'

Graham turned away while he tried to puzzle it out. Then once more facing his companion, he seemed to himself to risk everything in a single question: 'Why were you sent home?'

Brocklehurst just perceptibly coloured. 'You haven't, you know, considering that you are my friend, a very overwhelming confidence in me.'

Graham looked down. 'Yes, I have,' he answered suddenly, impulsively. 'You must forgive me. I am a pretty low kind of chap to have ever doubted you; but I'll never do so again.'

'Not even if another fellow comes along and tells you things?'

'Never, so long as I live. . . . What a beast you must think me.'

Brocklehurst shook his head. 'I only think that some one has been doing his best to turn you against me. I dare say it is natural enough. . . . You see, I used to get out at night—not very often, but now and again—and they didn't understand.'[32]

'Get out?'

'Yes; through one of the windows. . . . And because I didn't take anybody into my confidence, they were sure I was up to no good. . . . I *had* to go. . . . I can't explain.'

'You mean, it *wasn't* to do any harm?'

'It was only to be out there—to breathe the air, to be under the sky.'

'But in the daytime—couldn't you——'

'No. I wanted to run in the moonlight; to run over the meadows; to bathe in the river; to be free.'

'But why didn't you tell them—when you knew what they thought?'

'Oh, they are welcome to their thoughts. I've never in my life explained any of my actions, and I'm not going to begin now. Do you know——?' he hesitated.

'Know what?'

'Only a strange fancy I used to have at such moments. It was rather queer'—he smiled shyly. 'I used to feel just as if I had gone back to the life I had always been accustomed to—as if I had just awakened, if you can understand—while the other, my ordinary life, appeared to be a kind of dull dream, a kind of captivity which I should have to return to, but which, nevertheless, was not real.'

Graham watched him a moment in silence. 'Suppose—suppose your fancy were the truth!'

'The truth! Oh, nonsense! How could it be?'

'Suppose you really did, long ago, live a life like that!'

'Among woods and meadows and streams?'

'Long ago, long ago——'

Brocklehurst shook his head.

'The grass was soft under your feet,' Graham whispered dreamily, 'and there was the humming of bees——"

'Where?—Where do you mean?'

'And you played on the flute of Pan;[33] and you bathed in the streams. . . . Do you remember?'

'It was there that we first met?'

'It was there that we ran in the sunlight over the green grass.'

'It was there that we lay in the shadow of the trees.'

'The deep sea: the dark sky: the sunshine: the waving branches: the garden:—it is just as if I could see the reflection of them all in your eyes. . . . *Do* you remember?'

Brocklehurst shook his head again. 'Only when you tell me,'—he laughed somewhat ruefully. 'After all, it is *your* garden, you know. I can't get there by myself.'

'If we really could get there!'

'Oh, well, I'll come with you any time if you'll show me the way.'

'Suppose you had a dream,' Graham said slowly, thoughtfully, 'and in your dream you saw there was only *one* way—should you have the courage to take it? I mean, if it was a way that seemed to lead into the darkness?—death!'

'Death!' Brocklehurst looked at him as he repeated the word. 'No,' he half whispered, 'not that—I hate the idea of it. I hate everything connected with it.'

'Still——'

'Have you ever seen a dead person?'

'No.'

'I have, then—once. . . . I was made to look. . . . It was my grandfather. . . . But I'll never look again at anything of that kind—never—never—never. . . . He was so changed—you can't think. . . . His face and hands were like wax. . . . His hands. . . . Oh, I didn't like them. . . . I saw them that night after I had gone to bed . . . they were on the bedclothes . . . they came closer and closer . . . it was horrible. . . . No, no, there was no garden for him, believe me!—nothing—nothing any more.'

VI

ND it seemed to Graham that nowhere, save only in a few poems, and in one or two passages of Plato, he could find the expression of a sentiment even approximating to that he felt for his friend. Many books he turned over, and such lines as caught his fancy he read again and again until he knew them by heart. Those portions of the *Sonnets* of Shakespeare which were least rhetorical, which appeared to spring from a genuine feeling, he learned in this way. Was not *his* friend, too, the 'lord of his love,' the 'herald of the spring,' the 'lovely boy,' the 'rose of beauty,' 'music to hear'?—[34]

> 'For all that beauty that doth cover thee
> Is but the seemly raiment of my heart.'

And again:—

> 'Shall I compare thee to a summer's day?
> Thou art more lovely and more temperate:
> Rough winds do shake the darling buds of May,
> And summer's lease hath all too short a date:
> . . . .
> But thy eternal summer shall not fade.'

Nevertheless, it was in two poems by Rossetti, two poems of unsurpassable beauty, *The Stream's Secret* and *Love's Nocturn*,[35] that he found, or thought he found, what

he himself actually felt; their suggestion of a kind of impassioned mysticism appealing to him, being indeed but
an echo of that curious vein of mysticism which from
the first had entered into and made more wonderful his
own love. These poems, altering the gender of the personal pronouns, and thinking of Harold while he said
them, he repeated over and over to himself, until in the
end they became in his mind so bound up with his friend
that he could not have imagined them in any other connection, that he could not have heard them without see-
ing Harold's face.

The spring passed quickly; summer was already here;
and as Graham, fallen now completely into the ways of
his new life, watched one day after another glide swiftly
from him, sometimes he longed to stretch out his hand
to stay this or that particular hour and keep it with him
for ever.

On an afternoon in the beginning of July he had
flung himself down in the shade, and was lying on his
back among the long, sweet-smelling grass. He had been
fielding out for more than an hour under a deep, cloud-
less sky, and he was a little tired and hot. His straw hat
lay on the ground beside him, and he gazed up at the sky
through the leafy branches of a tree that stretched above
him like a gigantic parasol. The delicious summer heat,
the stillness, made him feel rather drowsy; and he let
his thoughts wander hither and thither on the wings of
every idle fancy. Already the shouts from the cricketers
reached him only as a far-off murmur, blended dreamily
in his mind with the humming of a great black and yellow striped bee, which flitted noisily from cup to cup of
a group of purple fox-gloves growing close at hand.

Days like this were very beautiful, he thought, and this old volcanic earth with its bright delicate covering, like a carpet, of grass and trees and flowers. And life!—yes; and life itself was beautiful! For the same life that was moving joyously within his young warm blood, was moving in the sap of tree and grass. What was it all? Whence did it spring? Every day a miracle was wrought when some delicate leaf, or the spiral of a new-born fern, unfolded itself in the soft air, or pushed up through the dark clinging soil. And this was life! And he was alive! He found an exquisite happiness in the thought that he himself was thus a part of nature, so close to nature in her simpler forms. It was as if—always alive to the charm of such things—he understood now for the first time the full meaning of the old Greek 'tree-worship,' realised, as it were, its origin, in his own emotions. That faculty for noting the listening soul, the spirit that is in leaf or plant, seemed to be a part of his very human nature, seemed as some ancient bond of relationship that bound him then, and would bind him for ever, to stiller and less perfect forms of life—to a whole world of pastoral divinities—the great god Pan himself; the Hamadryads, who inhabit the forest trees; and Oreads, and Naiads, and Hyades—the deities of water-springs, and streams, and showers of summer rain.[36]

As he thought of it a wave of joy seemed to raise him up suddenly on its strong, full flood; a deep happiness that had come to him often before in his solitude, and which, for the time at any rate, was sufficient. To live! to live! to live! it seemed to cry—that was enough; there was nothing else in the world. Ah, surely he must be happy so long as the sun shone and all nature sang with that great rhythmic chaunt of sensuous life! He closed his eyes that the exquisitely fresh and living smell of the earth, his mother, the cool sweet green smell of the swaying grass, might creep into his very being. How delicious it was just to lie there in the lush green grass, among the clear, floating shadows—to lie and think his thoughts as they drifted into his mind from the outer sunshine.

When he chose to look in their direction, he could see his schoolfellows eager still over their game of cricket; but he was content to watch them, content to look on, lazily, dreamily, through his half-closed eyelids, following every now and then the swift curving passage of the ball through the air, when it rose above the fielders' heads.

And in everything, though in a somewhat misty fashion, he seemed to feel the personality, the influence, of Harold Brocklehurst. Was it not all—his extraordinarily vivid sense of life—bound up in some subtle way with the beauty of their friendship? Had not their friendship helped him to realise the mystery and loveliness of nature; helped him to make things out; helped to unseal his eyes? It was the force of a temperament that found expression very easily, which he felt to be working now upon his own simpler nature, his spirit, his mind,—altering everything around him, awakening a new beauty in familiar things, suggesting a wider, deeper, more mystical beauty where before he had only been conscious of a material impression. It carried with it, too, a hundred hints, memories, of a strangely familiar paganism, of a fresher, younger world; a hundred touches of poetry:—the sun, the climbing plant: Apollo, Dionysus:—

strong, beautiful, swift. This boy!—what had he to do
with them? Why should he suggest them? And then, in
the background, a haunting sense of something darker,
more fateful—tragic even!—again the legend of Dionysus;[37] but more pitiable, quite human, vaguely pathetic
and bewildering.

By and by he opened a copy of the *Phaedrus*, which
he had worked through with his father, and began to
read.

They had studied together most of the shorter dialogues, and the whole of the *Republic*, but the *Phaedrus*
Graham cared for most. In its pages he had taken his first
peep at philosophy—philosophy, as conceived by him,
so near to, so replete with, poetry;—'Really, Phaedrus,
you make a most charming guide.'[38] Nay, it *was* poetry!
deep, impassioned poetry! for with Plato, even the trees
and streams, all the lovely things of the visible world,
were made to play their parts. It was as if they possessed
active and living souls. They had at least, the boy felt, a
wonderful share in the development of one's *own* soul:
they seemed to breathe about it an atmosphere of light
and purity and happiness. In Plato's philosophy—so far
as he understood it—there was little he could not accept.
On one very hot, still day, for instance, a passing breath
of wind on his face had suddenly awakened in him the
recollection of a prior existence—faintly, vaguely, perhaps, but still quite clearly enough to stamp a definite
impression on his mind.

And for him, of all writers, this old Greek had the
most delightfully personal charm. As he read him, indeed, it seemed as if the peculiar beauty of his nature
were exhaled gently from the printed pages—gently and

very delicately—like, say, the faint perfume of a spray of
sweet-briar he had dried a few days ago between them,
and which now as he came suddenly upon it and held it
to his lips, breathed still the ghostly shadow of its former
fragrance. Surely no other books were so fair and sweet,
so wise and true. In the charmed circle of their range,
the coarser qualities of things were forgotten, the light
was cleansed, the whole realm of the soul lay clear. He
knew no other writings that flowed in with so gracious a
charm upon one's spirit, filling it with a love for all that is
beautiful and good, watering its 'wing-feathers': no others that exercised so humanising an influence upon one's
character. For it was, in truth, before all else, a philosophy of life, of the highest life one may hope to lead here
upon earth, or later on in heaven. A philosophy of love,
too, necessarily!—and of beauty. Of all earthly things
beauty approximated most nearly to its eternal idea: and
love!—well, all desire for good and happiness, nay, even
the working of philosophy itself—all that was only the
gracious power of love. On these the path was builded,
the Platonic ladder reaching from earth to heaven; for
one climbed, after all, to those pure, colourless regions,
to that radiant world of ideas, by Phaedo's golden hair.

Well! such a doctrine met most of the needs of his
own spirit, and awakened in him, naturally, a very friendly feeling for its author; the kind of affection we have for
any one who has thought just the same thought, felt just
the same joy or sorrow, that we are thinking and feeling
now. As a young boy will linger long beside some deep
pool of sea-water he finds among the rocks, peering
down into its minute caverns and among its seaweeds for
unknown curiosities and treasures, so Graham lingered

over these pages, trying to learn all things from them, a rule of life for himself, a rule whereby he might, as far as was possible, enter into and judge the lives of others, might discover what to cling to, what to throw away. Over the dark still well of Life he leaned, and through that deep cool water, ruffled gently by the soft warm breath of youth, the face of Love himself arose, his hair streaming back like a flame, his sad grey eyes full of an infinite pity.

And he began to dream of an immortal love which, though unable to realise itself perfectly in this world, yet might be strong enough to draw two souls together, after death, in some far heaven. Far! But in truth it seemed quite near just now:—was here, a soft radiance, in his own spirit, in the warm air that blew about his face, in the sunlight, in the trees, in the voices of his playmates. Only afterwards—afterwards there would be that untroubled and perfect communion which hovered now before him as an unattainable ideal, a light behind the clouds, a flame on the horizon; 'for then, and not till then, the soul will be parted from the body and exist in herself alone.'[39]

Plato's theories blew just like a cool wind upon the dust gathered in one's mind. They entered one's mind easily and at once, sinking down into the very depths of one's spirit, to be a light there for ever, to sing there for ever, as the morning stars sang together.

And they were so bound up with ordinary existence, with the affairs of every day! They stretched out from their idealism a friendly hand to which he could cling when struggling along the rough muddy roads of the world. But above all, he was charmed with the theory of natural suggestion, the influence beautiful things have upon one in childhood and boyhood in the building-up and equipment of one's character. The grouping of clouds about a sunset, the noise of running water—these, and other things like these, were working always, working delicately, upon one's mind and temper, shading them, as it were, to fairer colours and softer outlines. For material beauty is at least one rung, though it be the lowest, in the Platonic ladder. Higher fair souls; fair virtues higher still; and highest of all the pure idea of Beauty itself, invisible to the eye of sense, but lying bright and clear before the vision of the mind, a glorious sight, to be viewed by those alone who have cleansed their souls of earthly passions:—'Blessed are the pure in heart, for they shall see God.'[40]

When he had finished the little introduction he closed the book and laid it upon the grass beside him. Nothing he had ever read, he thought, called up more vividly the impression, the very sound and smell of life out of doors. In each word was an exquisite suggestion of nature, of the open air, of the trees and green grass, and the cool shallow stream up which Socrates and Phaedrus had walked.[41] The spirits that had haunted the bank under the plane-tree seemed now to haunt the pages of the dialogue. And indeed, as though magically changed, the elm above him had suddenly become a plane-tree. Nay! he could hear, actually hear, the trickle of the stream—could hear the chirping of the grasshoppers. And Phaedrus and Socrates!—yes, Phaedrus and Socrates were talking still: if he listened very intently he could make out the tones of their voices, even their words—if he closed his eyes he could see them.

'Beloved Pan, and all ye other gods who haunt this place, give me beauty in the inward soul; and may the outward and inward man be at one. May I reckon the wise to be the wealthy, and may I have such a quantity of gold as a temperate man and he only can bear and carry.—Phaedrus, need we anything more? The prayer I think is enough for me. . . .'[42]

The sounds about him drew farther and farther away as though fading back into dreamland. A clear light, pale green, like a reflection from some deep pool, was in the sky. The whole world was changed, and he seemed to be wandering in a country of gentle streams and meadows, while the green grass was gay with yellow daffodils.

The sunlight slanted lower, falling on the upper windows of the school. Was his dream less real than that soft light, he wondered? Did not both come from somewhere in the clouds? It explained so much; it pushed back, as it were, the horizon. Plato had believed in it. Could it be, then, that there were certain persons—like Plato, like himself—who were actually nearer to the unseen than others were?[43] Surely things came to him, with the scent of flowers, with the sighing of wind, with the splash of the sea! There was a spirit which breathed upon him from the rustling trees and from the grass under his feet.

VII

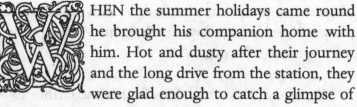

HEN the summer holidays came round he brought his companion home with him. Hot and dusty after their journey and the long drive from the station, they were glad enough to catch a glimpse of the house when yet some distance away. And as the evening sun, washing the beeches with soft red-gold, fell obliquely on the upper windows, the effect for the young visitor was one of a singularly peaceful beauty, such as he had never before known. Standing back among the trees in the midst of that green terraced garden—a house of stillness and of charm—to him it appeared to be, as indeed it was, cut off completely from the outer world—the world, at least, as it had been for him; a London life, a hurried, anyhow existence when he joined his people in the holidays.

For Graham, also, to be home here once more was very pleasant. They dined in the great oak dining-room—the light of sunset streaming in across the table, catching the whiteness of damask, the deep crimson of roses half buried in their dark green leaves, the gleam of glass and old silver, and making the shaded candles to be but ornamental. On the dark panelled walls hung a few choice Dutch 'genre' paintings:—an 'Interior,' by Pieter de Hooch; a 'Music Lesson,' by Gerard Terburg; a 'Frost Scene,' by Adriaen van de Velde; a 'Portrait,' by Gerard Dou;[44] but no picture, Graham thought, could ever be half so charming as the young boy sitting opposite him, the softly blended light playing upon his beautiful face, his delicate hands. Graham watched him with a curious feeling of pride. He noticed his delightful courteousness, his perfect breeding, his wonderful distinction. Yes, there was a great deal in birth, in blood![45] For even in his short experience of school life he had learned something of the hopelessness and vulgarity of a spreading democracy. And he saw with pleasure that his father had taken to the boy, that he was not insensible to the deference of Harold's manner, his efforts to please, his easy grace.

After dinner the two boys wandered out of doors again, but went no further than the porch. Both were a little tired. Brocklehurst sat on one of the steps, and Graham half sat, half lay, a little below him, tracing with the point of a stick fantastic lines and figures in the gravel of the carriage sweep. The quiet of evening, of the perfect ending of a day, was all about them; and they sat in silence, that strange silence which seems to listen for the faint footfall of the hour that is approaching, the hour that is to be, the hour as yet so full of mystery, of hope, of the unknown.

The lawn stretched below them, smooth, greyish in the waning light. Upon its shaven surface clumps of laurel, barbary, and rhododendron stood out as darker, bordering patches—stood out a little stiffly in the nearly windless air; and against the clear pale sky the trees of the avenue were still.

'How close that cloud is!' Graham murmured. 'Isn't it almost as if we ourselves were floating up to it?'

Yet notwithstanding the dreaminess of his mood,

his senses were curiously alert. Remote sounds and faint perfumes reached him, which at another hour he would not have been conscious of. And he noticed Brocklehurst's hands as they rested on the stone step: he noticed the fineness of the skin, darkened to a rich golden-brown by the sun; the tapering fingers; the tiny blue vein, scarce visible, on the inside of the wrist. His hands were extraordinarily living, extraordinarily sensitive, expressive. They seemed made to touch the strings of musical instruments, to play upon some delicate lute or viol. He imagined that they must have some power in them to allay pain; he imagined them, cool and soothing, laid softly upon his own forehead, or over his mouth and eyes.

And suddenly Harold began to speak. 'It is very quiet here. . . . How strange you must have found everything when you first came to school!—after having been accustomed to this for so long.'

Graham smiled lazily. He felt very happy. It was as though a day he had long awaited had at last begun to break within his spirit, as though some perfect hour of life were here. And his present gladness was mingled somehow with all the happiness that had been before; with all the happiness he had ever known. He watched the dark leaves scarce tremulous against the sky; he watched the dark grass, the gathering dusk everywhere; the night wind was soft upon his face.

The light grew more and more subdued; the outlines of things vaguer and vaguer.

'I cannot tell you how glad I am to have you here, Harold,' he whispered shyly.

'It was very good of your father to ask me.'

'To ask you! But it all belongs to you! It has all been waiting for you for so long—and now, at last, you have come.' He spoke half-laughingly, but all his childish imaginings and dreams were stirring within him.

'How dark it is getting!'

The last glimmer of twilight had in truth died out of the sky, and only a dim pallor seemed to hang in the air, a faint reflection from the hidden moon.

'Listen!'

'It is my father. He plays to himself every evening; he is very fond of music.'

The soft, clear notes of a violin were drawn out slowly across the stillness. The darkness, the charm of the night, helped to make them wonderfully expressive, and Brocklehurst almost held his breath to listen. When a pause came he gave a little sigh. 'Why is beautiful music always so sad?' he wondered; 'so much sadder than anything else?'

'Is it?' Graham asked. 'And yet you like it!'

'Yes; there is nothing else I like so well. . . . I used to sing in the choir at school until my voice broke; but I have never learned very much.'

Graham raised himself a little. He leaned his chin on his companion's shoulder and looked out into the darkness. And he felt Brocklehurst's soft, warm cheek against his own.

'You went to school when you were very young, Harold, didn't you?' he murmured.

'No younger than most fellows. You, you know, came particularly late.'

'My father liked to have me here . . . I have not been at school a year yet . . . but all those other years before I

went seem very far away. I can look back at the past as if
it had only been a single hour. Everything slips together
into one golden point. . . . I wonder if, when a man is
dying, it is like that—if, when he looks back, all his life
gathers together into one long, long day—if all seems
but a summer day—yesterday between sunrise and
sunset——'

VIII

RADUALLY, as he rowed, the familiar landmarks grew smaller and the scene widened out, while the sprinkling of little cottages slid closer together. Beyond these, the spire of the church rose like a slender thread into the dark blue sky.

Brocklehurst's eyes rested upon his face, but he appeared to be quite unconscious of this, his own dark grey eyes fixed on some point in the remote.

At length he drew in his oars.

How far away the land seemed! All around, sea—sea unspotted by a single sail—sea stretching from world to world.

He lay back in the bow of the boat, and for a time appeared to have fallen into one of those reveries his companion knew so well.

And Brocklehurst began to murmur to himself while he dabbled his hand in the water.

'What?—What do you say?' At the sound of his friend's voice breaking through the fine meshes of his dream, Graham roused himself and made a movement to sit up.

Brocklehurst smiled. 'Nothing—nothing. I was only talking to myself.'

Graham looked at him. 'Doesn't it seem as if we were quite out of the world here, Harold? We shall never be more alone together than we are now. I can hardly remember when we came. . . . Do you think we shall ever go back?'

'Perhaps the sea round Ireland is haunted, like the sea of the Ancient Mariner.'[46]

'And the sea across which Odysseus sailed. Surely almost every place is haunted by this time. If we rowed on a little further we might come to Circé's Island,[47] or to the land of the Lotus-eaters,[48] or to the home of Nausicaa.'[49]

And even while he spoke they seemed to drift into a stiller air—or was it his fancy? His thoughts seemed to be borne into his mind from somewhere far away, and the faint lapping of the water against the boat recalled to him his dream.

'Last night I went back there, Harold—I found the old way. . . . Shall I tell you? . . . You remember the curious dream that filled up so much of my life here. . . . I think it must be beginning to open out again.'

'You mean about the boy whom you used to fancy as being in some way connected with me?'

Graham met his eyes. 'Are you quite sure he wasn't?' he asked softly. 'You must tell me, because just now, somehow, I am not quite certain myself.'

'What has changed you, then? You used, you know, to be sufficiently sure. . . . Do you remember the day I found you out in the fields?'

'The day you came to me? . . . You came when I called.'

'Well, you were very certain then, weren't you?' He laughed a little at the other boy's gravity.

'That was the beginning,' Graham murmured. 'Do you know that from that day until last night I have never dreamed of you, nor of the place where I used to find you . . . never till last night.'

'And last night you *did*?'

Graham glanced up at his companion. 'It all came back,' he answered simply. 'You were there—just as before I went to school—but changed—a little changed.' He tried to remember. 'I can't exactly say what the difference was,' he went on slowly, turning it over in his mind. Then he paused, in his effort to puzzle it out. '*Why* should you have come back?—after so long, I mean. Why, if you *were* coming, should you not have come sooner?'

'Ah, I can't tell you,' smiled Brocklehurst. 'Perhaps if you had asked me last night——!'

'You would have told me? . . . You did tell me, but I don't remember what you said. Somehow it has all grown very dim. Your being with me here, I think, has thrown the other back.'

'But wasn't it to tell you something that I returned?'

A peculiar, half-baffled expression passed across Graham's face. 'I thought I was going to remember,' he sighed, 'but it has gone again. . . . I suppose I shall never know now.'

'Ah, well, I can't help you any further.' Brocklehurst watched him with some amusement.

'No.' He sighed again. Then he looked across once more at his companion. 'As soon as I fell asleep I saw him—my dream-boy. I awoke, it seemed, on the seashore, at the very gate of his garden. And I heard his voice calling me—calling, calling. . . . Oh, I remembered his voice so well! I opened the gate, and he was there.'

He paused a moment, and his eyes grew dark with a strange shadow. And it was through this shadow that his next words seemed to drop, his voice becoming lower and lower, till at length it was scarce audible, scarce more than a whisper.

'Who he is, what he is; if he indeed be your spirit, or if you only remind me of him, I suppose I shall never know. At times I think he must have been born with me, and have grown with the growth of my soul. Until I went to school, at any rate, as I have already told you, he was my only playmate. When I was a little boy I used to pretend he was in the garden with me, and I used to look for him here and there, just as if he were hiding from me in some game. . . . At night, I remember, when I had got into bed I used to wonder where he was just then, and if he would be waiting for me when I woke up in his country. And he always *was* waiting—standing there patiently, smiling, ready to welcome me. . . . Now and then I even went to bed earlier than usual, to see if I could by any chance get there before him; but I never could, because, I suppose, he lived there. . . .

'And last night—I don't know why—it was just the same. Everything happened as in the old days. . . . It is rather strange, for of late it had all grown a little dim and far away—faint, unreal even, when I tried to bring it back. . . . And I remember he took me to the edge of a pool, and when I looked into the water I saw reflected there my own room—a boy lying asleep in the bed— myself——'[50]

He paused, smiling faintly, his whole face filled with the light of his memory. Brocklehurst watched him curiously.

'Sometimes,' he went on, 'sometimes the wind, when it is not too loud, seems to bring back the sound

of his voice . . . and his voice is just like yours, Harold.
. . . Once, at school, I remember, I was sitting before
the fire, half asleep and half awake, when suddenly he
seemed to come very close to me, to be in the room, to
be leaning over the back of my chair. Then I shut my
eyes and I felt his soft hair brush against my cheek—and
I waited—and oh, I felt so happy. . . . All at once the door
opened and you came in. . . . And you leaned over my
chair just as he had done, while you talked to me.'

'You are making me feel very jealous,' said Brocklehurst with pretended seriousness. 'I expect you like him
much better than you like me!'

'There is no difference . . . except——' He stopped
short while Brocklehurst began to laugh.

'Well, what were you going to say?'

Graham coloured a little. 'Let us change places. You
can row back.'

Brocklehurst obeyed him, but he still kept his eyes
fixed on Graham's face. 'What is the difference?' he persisted. 'What were you going to tell me?'

'Nothing—nothing,' Graham answered almost con-
fusedly. 'It is just in his—his manner.'

'That means, I suppose, that he *is* nicer—after all!'

'No, it doesn't mean anything of the kind.'

'Well, it must mean something, you know. And if
not that, why are you afraid to tell me?'

'I'm not afraid to tell you. . . . It means just that he
likes—me.' He gazed down through the water.

Brocklehurst regarded him a little strangely. For
a moment he seemed about to speak, but in the end,
without saying anything, he dipped his oars and began
to row back.

A long silence followed.

'Where shall we go now?' Brocklehurst asked gently. The boat was heading for the cliffs, which rose, dark and naked, out of the clear water.

'There is a place a little to the left where I think we can land if you would care to bathe.'

Brocklehurst brought the boat round to the desired spot, and they scrambled out on to a broad flat shelf of rock where, having made fast the rope, they sat for a while dangling their feet over the edge.

The sunlight made the water very clear and tempting. Floating faintly through the still afternoon came the notes of the church clock. From everywhere the salt, invigorating smell of seaweed just uncovered by the ebb tide was blown into their faces, and long trailing branches of it, golden-brown and grass-green in the sunlight, rose and sank with the swell. Here and there, a little lower down, sprays of a brighter colour were visible—pink and red and orange, like delicate, feathery coral.

'This place and this weather are pleasant enough for Pan,' Graham murmured. 'Next month it will be all over, and we shall be going back to school. I wonder if it will ever be just so nice again.'

After their bathe they sat on the rocks, baking in the hot sun. 'How brown your hands and face and neck are!' said Graham lazily. 'The rest of you seems so white. . . . I wonder if the Greeks ever made a statue of a diver? I don't remember one.' Then a sudden thought seemed to strike him and he sprang to his feet, his drowsiness suddenly gone. 'Wait a moment,' he cried. 'Stand there. . . . Turn round just a little. . . . You must lean against the rock and hold this bit of seaweed in your hand; and you must cross your feet—like that. Oh! if you just had pointed ears, or the least little bit of a tail! . . . A Faun! A Faun! A young woodland Faun! . . . You are far nicer than the statue.'[51] And a look almost of wonder came into Graham's face.

Next, making him sit down, he put him in the posture of the 'Spinario,' his old favourite; and then, raising him to his feet once more, he made him stand like the praying boy of the Berlin Museum, the 'Adorante,' his face and hands uplifted to the joy of the morning.[52]

'And now what else?' he murmured. 'You are too young for an athlete. Your body is too slender. I will make you into a youthful Dionysus instead. Let me put this seaweed in your hair. It is a wreath of vine.'

He placed him so that he leaned against the black, smooth rock, and the soft melting lines of the boy's body shone out with an extraordinary beauty from the sombre background.[53] Graham paused for a moment, and stepping back, shaded his eyes with his hand while he gazed fixedly at his work. A faint colour came into his cheeks and he advanced again. Very gently he pulled the brown waving hair over the boy's forehead, and a little lower still, giving to his face a more feminine oval, like that of Leonardo's 'Bacchus.'[54] He pulled his head, too, slightly forward, bending it from the shapely neck; and with delicate fingers he half lowered the lids of the dark, clear blue eyes, till the upper lashes, long and curling, cast a shadow on the cheek below; and he parted the lips, ever so softly, till a strange dreamy smile seemed to play upon them.

The accuracy of his touch almost startled him, and his colour deepened as the boy's beauty flowed in upon him, filling him with a curious pleasure. He laughed aloud. 'You are just like one of the young gods,' he cried. 'I wonder if you really are one. Perhaps if we stay much longer we shall draw the others down from heaven.'

'Isn't that what you would like? I expect you still, deep down, have a kind of faith in them.'

'Ah, how can I help having faith when one stands living before my eyes? All hail, dear Dionysus! child of fire and dew, and the creeping, delicate vine! . . . Should we not offer up a sacrifice, Harold? I have nothing here but these dry sea-flowers which I gathered from the rock, but it is into the heart of the giver, and not at the gift, that the gods look. . . . Let us offer our slender garland to the presiding deity of the place.'[55]

He knelt down, and laid the few sea-pinks, and the seaweed with which he had adorned his friend, on a little shelf of rock. 'That is the altar,' he said smiling, but more than half serious. Then he took Brocklehurst's hand and pulled him down to kneel beside him while he prayed.

'What god shall I give them to?' he whispered. 'You see they have so few worshippers left that they may be a little jealous of one another. We do not want the waves to rise up against us as they rose against Hippolytus.'

'Give them to the unknown God.'[56]

'Hush!—they will hear you: they must be drawing very near.—O gods of Hellas![57] If anything in our lives have found favour in your sight, accept this, our gift, which, though it be poor, is given with our love; and we beg that you will grant to each of us that thing which may be best for him. . . . Harold, "need we anything more? The prayer, I think, is enough for me."'

IX

HE could not quite say how it had happened. It had come so suddenly, so suddenly. And now, a few steps behind the others, he was walking toward the house. He had a feeling of sickness, of horror: a helpless misery, the meaning of which he shrank from realising, darkened his mind. Only he remembered—he could not help remembering: it was there before him with a curious vividness—the light of the afternoon sun on the long white road; the glare, the heat, something dark and motionless stretched in the dust—still, very still. . . .

Brocklehurst had been walking a few paces behind him, and close to the hedge. He had been pulling some wildflowers—a few had been scattered about him as he lay there on the road, so strangely quiet and white, a thin stream of red blood creeping through his hair and widening out, forming a little patch of mud. . . . And when he had lifted him, the curious whiteness of his face!

Yet in a way he had escaped wonderfully. None of the wheels had touched him: just that single kick a little above his left ear. . . .

They had been walking slowly, Brocklehurst close to the hedge, he, Graham, in the middle of the road, when the terrified horses had come dashing round the corner, the drag swaying violently behind them, one of the reins hanging broken and useless. He remembered jumping to one side. His foot had slipped on something, and he had fallen. The dust, the noise, a wheel just touching his coat as he rolled himself out of the way. . . . He knew now that Brocklehurst had sprung at the horses' heads, had given him, it might be, that one extra moment. . . .

And now it was all over. Their long afternoon in the boat; on the rocks; their little act of pagan worship;—all that had been *this* afternoon, and it was over. He was walking, a few steps behind the others, up the avenue toward the house.

X

IGHT at last.

Every one at length gone away; everything arranged; the house still and solemn.

His father had left him alone for a little with the dead boy. At last! . . .

His sorrow, which before the strangers he had kept swallowed down, he need hide no longer. There was no one to hear, no one to see. And he knelt beside the bed and stroked the smooth cold cheek. He kissed the cold mouth and stroked the soft dark hair from which all stain had been washed; and he put his arms about the body. And he remembered the boy as he had stood before him that afternoon in all his wonderful beauty. His tears fell fast and blindingly. The sobs rising to his throat almost choked him.[58]

XI

AY followed day. Brocklehurst had been buried in the village churchyard; his father and one of his brothers (all of his family who had come over) were returned home again; the blinds were drawn up; the quiet flow of life, so harshly and unexpectedly interrupted, had dropped back into its accustomed channel; only for one boy a light had gone out for ever from the sky; a glory and a beauty, as he had known them once, had vanished from the world.

All day long he tried to be alone, tried to avoid his father; and whenever an opportunity presented itself he would escape to his own room or to some solitary place out of doors. It was almost as if he were afraid of human companionship, afraid of the sound of his own voice. And a curious unwillingness to mention Harold's name, or to allude to him in any way whatever, seemed to have taken possession of him, though he spent daily a longer and longer time at the boy's grave, remaining there for hours, until his father, who knew of these visits, grew anxious for his health and wished to take him away from home, offered to take him abroad—France, Italy, Greece—anywhere he liked. But Graham pleaded so desperately to be allowed to stay where he was that Mr. Iddesleigh had not the heart to refuse him—feared, indeed, that in his present state of mind it might do him more harm than good.

Little wonder that the boy's health began to give

way; that he looked so pale and tired! The holidays were now almost over, but as yet nothing had been said about his going back to school, though Graham himself lived in secret dread of what he knew could not be put off for much longer. How, on the other hand, could he possibly resume the old life? The thought of what had been and never would be again—oh! that, he felt, he should not be able to bear—the dreariness, the loneliness, the hopelessness. Doubtless when he had first gone to school he had also been alone—but the difference, the difference now would be incalculable. There were days, in truth, when it almost seemed to him that it would have been better if he had never been given his happiness, since so soon it was to be snatched from him; and even though deep in his heart he knew he would not forget it if he could, there were days when he thought it would be well if all the past could be effaced from his mind, rubbed out as figures are rubbed from a child's slate.

One afternoon he was sitting with his father in the library. It had been raining for the greater part of the day, and a fine drizzle was still falling, though the sky was beginning to clear. It had been raining, and the soft sound of the rain—the soft, dripping sound, and the sight of the blurred landscape, had somehow a soothing effect upon him. On his knee he held an open book over which his head was bent closely. A lassitude, mental and physical, was visible in his every little movement, even in the way he sat; and between his eyes and the printed page he looked at, there floated a dead boy's face. A physical weakness weighed heavily upon him, a kind of stagnation of the very sources of his life, the

vital elements, sapping all power to rise above a certain
fixed and gloomy train of thought;—it was as if some
spring within him had been choked, dried up. . . . It was
finished!—finished!—finished! The word repeated itself
wearily in his mind, like the monotonous beating of a
metronome. He felt hot and feverish, and there was a
dull pain at the back of his head. It was almost as if he
were sickening for something. . . .

Tired out, for his sleep of late was become very restless and broken, presently he fell into a kind of doze,
from which he awakened, a few minutes later, to find his
father gazing anxiously at him; and with sudden contri-
tion he saw how selfish he had been in giving way thus
to his grief.

'Are you very tired?' Mr. Iddesleigh asked gently.
'Come over here and sit by me.' He drew his son to
him as he spoke, and Graham sat down on a stool at his
feet.

'What were you doing all this morning? Were you in
the cemetery?'

Graham nodded.

Mr. Iddesleigh laid his hand on the boy's head. 'You
go there so often!' he expostulated. 'It is not good for
you, Graham. What do you think about when you go
there all alone? What do you go there for?'

Graham hesitated. He clasped his hands about his
knees, while he sat gazing out of the window. The rain
had ceased and a pale sun was beginning to peep out between the heavy clouds. For some moments he did not
answer his father. The familiarity of everything about
him was borne into his mind. How often he and his father had sat just as they were sitting now!—in this same

room! It seemed to him that his life had been moving in a circle, and that he was beginning to return on a path he already knew. For a little the wings of some great spirit had drooped softly about his head. . . . 'Too like the lightning. . . . '[59] His eyes filled and he bent down to hide his face.

'What is the matter?' Mr. Iddesleigh asked, but still without getting any reply. 'Tell me, Graham, are you thinking about Harold?'

'Do you wonder I never speak of him?'

'Is it too near? . . . But your silence makes you brood over it all the more.'

'I cannot help thinking of him,' Graham whispered. 'He gave me his life.' He rose from his stool, and walking to the window pressed his forehead against the cold glass.

The rain was still dripping from the trees, and there was a damp smell in the air; but the sky was clearing, and the sun was growing stronger and stronger. Presently, and without further word, the boy left the room.

XII

OR a while he lingered near the house, restlessly, forlornly, but by and by he went down to the rocks, where he stood looking out over the sea.

Piled up on the horizon, like a vast range of purple-black hills, heavy masses of cloud drifted, scarce perceptibly, from east to west of the pale slate-blue sky; and where these rugged heaps were broken the heavens sank away in limitless wells of pure pale light, each edged with a border of bright grass-green. All the light of the day seemed gathered there—like a reflection from a world beyond—and Graham, as he stood at gaze before it, began to wonder if he should ever come any nearer to it than he was just there and then. In the *Phaedo* he had found many arguments for the immortality of the soul, but more lately he had realised, in his own life, the only one perhaps that actually counted—and this no argument at all; but merely a very simple human desire, a desire to look again upon the face of his friend, the face of him who was buried in the grave.[60]

He stooped down and leaned over the slowly-heaving water, watching it rise and sink back, and rise again and sink—over the dark, cold water that seemed nearly black against the rocks—lower still, and lower, till his hair almost brushed the surface.

'O water whispering
   Still through the dark into mine ears,—
As with mine eyes, is it not now with his?—
   Mine eyes that add to thy cold spring,
Wan water, wandering water weltering,
   This hidden tide of tears.'[61]

Presently he went on a little farther, clambering back
over the rocks, and taking a rough path which brought
him eventually to the church. The place was quite de-
serted, as it almost always was, and he pushed open the
gate. He walked over the soft grass till he came to Brocklehurst's grave, where he knelt down. The murmur of
the sea rose from below—monotonous, very peaceful.
Ah, were they not happiest who slept here with that dim
music drawing them farther and farther from the world?
An infinite melancholy drew its sombre wings about the
boy's forehead—a melancholy not wholly sprung from
his recent sorrow, but a kind of broader pity for all the
suffering bound up with life:—pity, above all, for the
young boy who lay now under the heavy earth, yet who
had once been so bright and active upon it. He found it
curiously hard to think of him as dead, out of existence.
Was he not still, even in that dim shadowy world whith-
er he had passed, conscious, sentient? Could he not still
feel some faint emotion, some faint stirring of hushed
joy or sorrow? Was not his heart still beating softly under the grass? He stretched himself upon the grave, lying full length, motionless. Face to face they lay, only
a little earth between them; and far below he seemed
to hear a breath drawn almost silently, to hear the slow,
sad stream of a boy's tears falling, falling evermore. In
the stillness he could hear his own heart beat—beat with

the life that was flowing away from him in a wide, clear flame, the flame of a lamp burning swiftly up into the night.

The sun had set when he turned to go home. But as he passed the church door he noticed that it stood ajar, and went in. A bucket of water and a broom were in the porch, left there evidently for some purpose; but the church itself was empty.

He sat down for a while in one of the pews; then he knelt, leaning his face between his hands. A strong desire to pray had come over him. But pray to whom? Was this then, at last, to be the hour of the unknown God? . . . And a few words floated into his mind, came to him again and again, like a memory of some old tune, or line of poetry: 'Little children, love one another . . .'⁶² It seemed as if some one were stooping down over him, it seemed as if some one had kissed him, kissed him softly, had laid a gentle hand upon his head.

And a feeling of ineffable peace began to creep into his heart. Could it possibly be, then, that he was really nearer to the unseen world than others were? Now, surely, in some inexplicable way he had been drawn very very close—closer than ever before. He had a sense that something was about to happen, and that it would be something great, momentous, supreme. It was as if he were upon the eve of some stupendous discovery; and he waited—waited till the signal should be given him—some sign which, unlike any others he had hitherto received, would come, this time, he knew, from without.

A profound stillness had fallen upon the church, like the closing in of heavy waters. The murmur of the sea had stopped.

Then across the hush there came a low sigh—a whisper as of the brushing together of innumerable leaves—a whisper which grew deeper and deeper, till at last it seemed the music of some wonderful summer, and Graham raised his head. Surely the light had grown marvellously clear and soft. A scent of many flowers was in the air; a murmur of a fountain.

And as he knelt, motionless, the walls of the church sank away from before him, and there—standing there in that radiance of perfect light—ah, there, at last, was Harold!

He stood in his garden, and he was more beautiful than Graham had ever yet beheld him . . . he stretched out his hands . . . he smiled. . . . His feet were pale on the dark rich grass with its powder of crocuses. Above his head the branches of the trees almost met, forming a delicate roof, a roof of green leaves, a green trellis very finely woven, through which the light, mingled with a falling music of little feathered throats, floated down soft and cool. All around him was that wonderful liquid light, and the music of water, listless, plashing, as it dropped into some dim, cool, green-lipped basin of stone. And over everything there hung a calm so deep, and pure, and holy, that all Graham's sorrow seemed to melt away before it into one impassioned sense of gratitude, and love, and peace.

'Oh, I am coming—I am coming,' he sobbed, rising to his feet, and taking a step forward, quickly, blindly. For a moment he stood there, swaying with a curious movement from side to side; then he gave a little moan and fell forward heavily on his face.

XIII

HEN he opened his eyes he was lying in bed, in his own room. The light was darkened: there was a faint smell of drugs in the air: and a figure was moving noiselessly about, preparing something at a small table. He had been ill, then! . . . but for how long?

He heard a slight noise as of the door being very carefully opened, and he saw his father come into the room, walking on tiptoe. Graham kept his eyes closed that they might not know he had awakened. Things were beginning to come back to him, and for just a few minutes longer he wanted to keep that cool darkness about him.

He felt a strange languor through all his body; he felt too weak to do anything but lie there in the softened light, and in the twilight of his soul. It would be soon enough to awaken in a little—not just yet—in a little. . . .

And all that was thirty years ago. His father was long dead. Every one was dead.

Dawn had crept into the room, grey and ghostly.[63] He shivered and looked round. His letter, unfinished, lay there on the table. Everything seemed cold, desolate, lifeless. He got up and stretched himself, for he felt stiff and cramped. Scarce worth while, now, to go to bed! He walked over to the window and looked out into the breaking day. The world seemed very old and cheerless. Was it the chill of approaching age in his own blood, he wondered, that made him find it so? He smiled a strange, dim little smile. Best, then, to sit by the fire and doze!

He came back to the table, and leaning over it, buried his face in his hands.

THE END

NOTES TO THE GARDEN GOD

[*Epigraph*]: Edgar Allan Poe, "A Dream Within a Dream," line 1. Since it is one of the keys to appreciating this short novel, the whole poem is reproduced below—from *The Poems of Edgar Allan Poe* (London: George Bell, 1900), p. 72:

> Take this kiss upon the brow!
> And, in parting from you now,
> Thus much let me avow—
> You are not wrong, who deem
> That my days have been a dream:
> Yet if hope has flown away
> In a night, or in a day,
> In a vision, or in none,
> Is it therefore the less *gone*?
> *All* that we see or seem
> Is but a dream within a dream.
>
> I stand amid the roar
> Of a surf-tormented shore,
> And I hold within my hand
> Grains of the golden sand—
> How few! yet how they creep
> Through my fingers to the deep,
> While I weep—while I weep!
> O God! can I not grasp
> Them with a tighter clasp?
> O God! can I not save
> *One* from the pitiless wave?
> Is *all* that we see or seem
> But a dream within a dream?

[*Epigraph*]: This is the last stanza of Dante Gabriel Rossetti's "Love's Nocturn" (see note 35 below).

[*Dedication*]: For ways in which this dedication proved fatal to any further relationship between Reid and James, see "Introduction," pp. xl-xlii.

1   Reid's choice of this surname certainly derived from William Allingham (1824-89), an Irish writer and a close friend and correspondent of Dante Gabriel Rossetti (1828-82), whose poetry plays a cardinal role in *The Garden God*—see George Birkbeck Hill, ed., *Letters of Dante Gabriel*

Rossetti to William Allingham, 1854-1870 (London: T. F. Unwin, 1897). This choice was further facilitated by the fact that Rossetti had provided illustrations for Allingham's volume of lyrical poems *Day and Night Songs* (1855) and for his *Flower Pieces and Other Poems* (1888). The former volume had, according to Reid, ushered in the "Golden age of wood-engraving," and he traces the history of this book in his *Illustrators of the Sixties*. The choice may have further sprung from one of Allingham's poems, "George; or The Schoolfellows," a poem that uses the word "dreamland" (in line 74)—one of the major themes of Reid's *Garden God*.

2   Graham's adherence to the philosophy of Epicurus is certainly mediated, as is much of Reid's early writing, through Walter Pater, particularly Pater's *Renaissance* and *Marius the Epicurean*. Consider the following passage from *Marius the Epicurean: His Sensations and Ideas*, Library edn, 2 vols (London: Macmillan, 1921 [1885]), I, p. 234:

> [Marius's] Cyrenaic philosophy, presented thus, for the first time, in an image or person, with much attractiveness, touched also, consequently, with a pathetic sense of personal sorrow:—a concrete image, the abstract equivalent of which he could recognise afterwards, when the agitating personal influence had settled down for him, clearly enough, into a theory of practice.

The Cyrenaic school of philosophy, which flourished in the city of Cyrene from about 400 to 300 BCE, was notable for its tenets of hierarchical Hedonism derived from Socrates and Protagoras. Late Cyrenaicism and Epicureanism are only distinguishable from each other in details, not fundamental principles, though, for Marius and for Pater, the distinct details that Epicurus held and advocated—that a proper knowledge of death makes one enjoy life the more, that wise men avoid taking part in public affairs, that one should not marry and beget children—were important. In *Walter Pater: Lover of Strange Souls* (New York: Knopf, 1995), Denis Donoghue glosses Pater's Cyrenaicism as "the assertion that the best way to live is to crowd as many pulsations as possible into one's inevitably brief life, and that the best way to do this is by cultivating art for art's sake" (p. 57).

3   Jacques Anatole Thibault (1844-1924), who used the pseudonym "Anatole France," was a prolific author who won the Nobel Prize in Literature in 1921.

4   Graham posits that one's "duties as a good citizen" include "to have married," which he has chosen not to do, claiming "I cannot, alas! even pretend that I want […] to forsake my wilderness." The homoerotic and pederastic connotations of this statement become more evident when

brought into proximity with E. M. Forster's "Terminal Note" (1960), appended to his novel *Maurice*, begun in 1913 (p. 221):

> Our greenwood ended catastrophically and inevitably. Two great wars demanded and bequeathed regimentation which the public services adopted and extended, science lent her aid, and the wildness of our island, never extensive, was stamped upon and built over and patrolled in no time. There is no forest or fell to escape to today, no cave in which to curl up, no deserted valley for those who wish neither to reform nor corrupt society but to be left alone.

This lack of interest in the "duties of a good citizen" was wide-ranging for Reid: "Still less was I susceptible to the charm of poems dealing with 'such topics as war, patriotism, prosperous love, religion, duty'—topics which I confess even to-day leave me cold" (Reid, *Apostate*, p. 186). In contrast to the spirit of the Irish Literary Revival, with its politicised poetics bountifully evident in the works of W. B. Yeats, J. M. Synge, and Sean O'Casey—in contrast to the defiance of The Great War poets, several of whom he knew personally, such as Rupert Brooke, or through contact with members of the Bloomsbury Set—Reid's continued maintenance of a Paterian antinomianism is rather surprising: "Reid did sustain a position of indifference towards questions of politics, whether they were Irish or of the wider world. Of the European War, Reid, who was thirty-nine at its outset, and exempt from conscription, made no mention, either of the hostilities or their effect on his writing" (Taylor, *Green*, p. 81). "As a novelist Mr. Forrest Reid stands above and apart from his Northern [Irish] contemporaries. Though he writes of Belfast life, he belongs to no school, and he is concerned with deeper things than the superficial differences which divide Ulster from their neighbours"—From a Correspondent, "Ulster's Share in the Revival," "Modern Literature," *The Times*, 5 December 1922, p. xviii.

5   The choice of this surname, "Iddesleigh" (pronounced "Idds-lee") is curious, perhaps ironical or comical. In 1898, Amanda McKittrick Ros (1860-1939), another Ulster writer, published *Irene Iddesleigh*, the first of a series of highly alliterative novels that have bestowed upon her lasting fame as "the worst novelist in English," with her audience unable to tolerate, without laughter, all those "touch tricks of the traitor, the tardy and the tempted," and "the retinue of retired rights, the righteous school of the invisible and the rebellious roar of the raging nothing." The Oxford literary group the Inklings, which included J. R. R. Tolkien, C. S. Lewis, Lord David Cecil, and other notables, had "an outstanding bet" involving whomever could read "a chapter of *Irene Iddesleigh* without a smile"—W. H. Lewis, *Brothers and Friends: The Diaries of Major Warren Hamilton Lewis*,

ed. by Clyde Kilby and Marjorie Lamp Mead (San Francisco: Harper & Row, 1982), p. 197.

6   "The old gardener only came once a week, for what sweeping and weeding needed doing; I was fain to learn to sweep the walks with him, but was discouraged and shamed by his always doing the bits I had done over again"—John Ruskin, *Praeterita* (London: George Allen, 1907), p. 75. This is probably one of the few passages that provides a link between Reid's childhood remembrances (whether fictively framed or in his autobiographical *Apostate*) and those detailed in Ruskin's *Praeterita*. Beyond their appreciation for the natural world, these two had nearly antipodal personalities, which might have inspired the choice of the name of the tutor—*Rusk*—in Reid's third novel, *The Bracknels: A Family Chronicle* (London: Edward Arnold, 1911).

7   "The slave-boy conversation is offered as an illustration of the theory of recollection"—H. H. Benson, "Meno, the Slave Boy and the Elenchus," *Phronesis*, 35.2 (1990), pp. 128-58 (p. 134). In "True Belief in the *Meno*," in *Oxford Studies in Ancient Philosophy*, vol. XIV, ed. by C.C.W. Taylor (Oxford: Oxford University Press, 1996), pp. 1-32, Panagiotis Dimas suggests instead that "[Plato] is telling us that to enlighten ourselves about recollection we must do exactly as Meno is asked to do. If a theory exists, we shall find it in the way the slave-boy finds the solution to the geometrical problem" (p. 3).

8   This seems a very loose translation of a passage from chapters 20-21 of "The Fourth Treatise" of *Il Convivio* (or *The Banquet*) by Dante Alighieri, a passage that seems to have sprung from the parables of "the good seed" in Matthew 13. This oft-ignored, fragmentary prosimetrum (a work composed of both verse and prose) had recently appeared as *The Convivio of Dante Alighieri*, trans. by Philip H. Wicksteed (London: The Temple Classics, 1903) and in the 3rd edition of the *Oxford Dante* (1904). In *Il Convivio: The Banquet of Dante Alighieri* (London: G. Routledge, 1887), Elizabeth Price Sayer translates this as:

> That seed of Happiness
>   Falls in the hearts of few,
> Planted by God within the Souls
>   Spread to receive His dew.
>
> [....]
>
> In Childhood they obey,
>   Are gentle, modest, heed
> To furnish Virtue's person with
>   The graces it may need.

Are temperate in Youth,
 And resolutely strong,
Love much, win praise for courtesy,
 Are loyal, hating wrong.

However, this "quotation" might instead be entirely a playful fabrication, since Reid was "fond of small practical jokes of a literary nature," as in fabricating quotations in other writers' styles, quotations that would then be erroneously attributed (for examples of such jokes, see Taylor, *Green*, pp. 157-58).

9 For the Victorians and the Edwardians, the most controversial, hence influential section of *The Renaissance: Studies in Art and Poetry* (titled *Studies in the History of the Renaissance* in the first edition) was its "Conclusion," a conclusion for which Pater later provided the following footnote (*Renaissance* 1893, p. 186):

> This brief "Conclusion" was omitted in the second edition of this book, as I conceived it might possibly mislead some of those young men into whose hands it might fall. On the whole, I have thought it best to reprint it here, with some slight changes which bring it closer to my original meaning. I have dealt more fully in *Marius the Epicurean* with the thoughts suggested by it.

The last passage of that "Conclusion" encapsulates Pater's elaborate *Weltanschauung*, and includes the passage that Reid quotes (p. 190, emphasis added):

> We are all under sentence of death but with a sort of indefinite reprieve— [. . .] we have an interval, and then our place knows us no more. Some spend this interval in listlessness, some in high passions, the wisest, at least among "the children of this world," in art and song. For our one chance lies in expanding that interval, in getting as many pulsations as possible into the given time. Great passions may give us this quickened sense of life, *ecstasy and sorrow of love*, the various forms of enthusiastic activity, disinterested or otherwise, which come naturally to many of us. Only be sure it is passion—that it does yield you this fruit of a quickened, multiplied consciousness. Of such wisdom, the poetic passion, the desire of beauty, the love of art for its own sake, has most. For art comes to you proposing frankly to give nothing but the highest quality to your moments as they pass, and simply for those moments' sake.

10 Besides that of the clergyman who presides over the Lowood Institution in Charlotte Brontë's *Jane Eyre* (1847), Brocklehurst is also the surname of a family in J. M. Barrie's *The Admirable Crichton: A Comedy* (1902).

11 In the commonplace book he kept in 1906, Reid relates a transcendental experience that he had had in front of a painting at The Royal Academy of Art, London (as quoted in Taylor, *Green*, pp. 42-43):

> It was in the summer of 1903 that a curious power of vision became more fully developed in me, and the first time that I became conscious of this was at the Academy exhibition of that year, where there was a picture that greatly attracted me, a portrait of a boy—Edward Meyerstein—painted by Storey.
>
> This boy is seated in a room. He has his right hand raised to his cheek, and his left hand is resting on an open book. Behind him, in the dimness, is the wall of the room, and what seems to be a case of stuffed birds is also faintly visible. He is dressed in loose untidy clothes, a tennis shirt, a gray jacket, and very wide trousers. He has a brown delicate skin, clear brown steadfast eyes, and waving hair. He is a beautiful boy, about sixteen years old, and I had been looking at the portrait for some time when a change came over it, gradual at first, and then quite rapid. The room in which the boy sat grew darker and the walls receded farther and farther till at last they vanished in a vast deep dun space that became a shadowy forest through which the boy, dressed now in a suit of pale silver and with a living light playing about his head, rode slowly toward me through the twilight. The hour was the dim "moth hour," the path was full of shadow, and roofed by branching trees. Behind, and glimmering palely from the shelter of gnarled trunks, vague phantoms watched and with no friendly gaze. But the boy rode on grave and fearless ... I tried now to see the original picture, but I could not, and something told me that I was looking on either the boy's innermost life, or on some former life of his, though I do not know exactly what my vision may mean.

12 This figure type, known as the *spinario* or *fedele* (*fedelino*) or thorn-puller, is most famously represented by a Hellenistic Greek bronze, dated 1st century BCE, in the Sala dei Trionfi, Museo del Palazzo dei Conservatori, Rome (Sixtus IV donation, 1471, MC1186). (A photograph of this sculpture appears as "Appendix Two.")

13 "What while Love breathed in sighs and silences / Through two blent souls one rapturous undersong"—Dante Gabriel Rossetti, "Youth's Antiphony" (lines 13-14), Sonnet XIII of *The House of Life*, in *The Collected Works of Dante Gabriel Rossetti*, ed. by William Michael Rossetti, 2 vols (London: Ellis and Scrutton, 1886), I, p. 183. "In poetry it was what was not said, what was communicated secretly, as in the whispering of spirit to spirit, that I valued" (Reid, *Apostate*, p. 188).

14 In his short story "Emerald Uthwart," in *Miscellaneous Studies: A Series of Essays*, 1st edn (London: Macmillan, 1895), pp. 170-214, Walter Pater's protagonist, the "gem-like" Emerald, is described as "a rather sensuous boy!" (p. 174), with qualities like those preferred and praised by Plato:

"conservative Sparta and its youth; whose unsparing discipline had doubtless something to do with the fact that it was the handsomest and best-formed in all Greece" (p. 182).

15 "Off [Achilles] went, the ghost of the great runner, Aeacus' grandson loping with long strides across the fields of asphodel, triumphant in all I had told him of his son, his gallant, glorious son"—Homer, *The Odyssey*, trans. by Robert Fagles (Harmondsworth, Middlesex, UK: Penguin, 1997), p. 267 (XI, lines 614-17).

16 "The thought that I was growing older tormented me too. I wanted to be a boy always; I would have given gladly the remainder of my existence to have had the past five years over again. [. . .] I clung to the fact that I was not yet seventeen" (Reid, *Apostate*, p. 218). This same dynamic would play out in various ways in his relationships with boys, as Brian Taylor relates (*Green*, pp. 98; 104):

> [Reid's] love admitted of little possibility of change, either in its strength or in its object. He did not relish the prospect of Kenneth [Hamilton]'s affection for him ever waning, even though that might come about by the boy's growing to manhood. If growing up meant growing away—as it had with Andrew [Rutherford]—then Kenneth had to be kept a little boy. And if that was not possible, then his memory at least had to be preserved static and unchanging.
>
> Better by far, as Reid already knew, to trust to memory to keep that small boy—"gay, responsive, affectionate and with the merriest laugh I have ever heard"—always young and unforgotten. At least Reid's memories of Kenneth, like the boy himself, could not grow up—or grow old.

17 Reid, *Apostate*, pp. 75-77:

> The part familiar to me was a kind of woodland, the turf for the most part short, and with many open glades and deep clear pools. In some of these glades were stone figures watching over our playground, and guarding it from intrusion. A spirit was alive within them: they could hear me and see me, though no breath passed their lips. And there was one different from all others [. . .] a crouching beast in black marble, with a panther's smooth body and a human face. [....]
>
> The dream itself, up to the end, remained *in* time, by which I mean that the boy in it grew older as I myself grew older. And then, somewhere about my sixteenth or seventeenth year, the whole thing was permanently cut off.

18 This is a reference to Arcadia, or the "dales of Arcady," as in John Keats, "Ode on a Grecian Urn," line 7. "The scene was there before me, strangely familiar, as if I were retracing my own footmarks in the sand. [....] [The scene included] a bright delicate company, young, beautiful,

gay, yet 'sad with the whole of pleasure.' Here were the brown faces, the pouting lips, and naked unspoiled bodies, the slim Pan pipes, the shadowed grass. [. . .] 'My world! My world!' I could have shouted [. . .] There—there—or nowhere. It was the only heaven I wanted, or ever was to want" (Reid, *Apostate*, pp. 27-28). "My deities were the Arcadian gods, the lesser gods, Pan and Hermes. [. . .] The deities I invoked, or evoked, were friendly, and more than half human; they were the deities of the poet and the sculptor" (pp. 210-11). It should be noted that Pater's most pederastic essay, "Winckelmann," in *The Renaissance*, has as its epigraph *Et ego in Arcadia fui*, literally "I too have been in Arcadia."

19   This should be interpreted, to some degree, within the context of Isaiah 14:12-14 (KJV): "How you are fallen from heaven, O Lucifer, son of the morning!"

20   "The Greeks thought that a dark complexion signified manliness, including virility and such manly virtues as courage [. . .]"—Page DuBois, *Centaurs and Amazons: Women and the Pre-History of the Great Chain of Being* (Ann Arbor, MI: University of Michigan Press, 1991), p. III.

21   This recalls, of course, Neverland in *Peter Pan*. Reid, *Apostate*, pp. 72-74:

> There were two worlds, and it never occurred to me to ask myself whether one were less real than the other. It did not seem to me that either was unreal, that either was my own creation. I lived in both, and the fact that I should open my eyes night after night in precisely the same spot in dreamland was no more surprising than that I should open them morning after morning in my bedroom at home. [. . . .]
>
> But *this* particular dreaming was pure happiness; and always the setting was the same, the time the same, the season the same [. . .] The place was a kind of garden. [. . . .] Meanwhile, I sat still, facing the wide blue glittering sea, and waited. [. . . .] I was waiting for someone who had never failed me—my friend in this place, who was infinitely dearer to me than any friend I had on earth. And presently, out from the leafy shadow he bounded into the sunlight. I saw him standing for a moment, his naked body the colour of pale amber against the dark background—a boy of about my own age, with eager parted lips and bright eyes. But he was more beautiful than anything else in the whole world, or in my imagination.
>
> Afterwards the dream might wander hither and thither; we might bathe in the sea or in one of the pools, or play upon the shore, or plunge into the woodland; we might be alone, or others might join us in a game; only the beginning was always the same, or very nearly the same.

22   As they depart together for Rome, Marius the Epicurean and Cornelius, who have only just met, begin a conversation that "left [them] with

sufficient interest in each other to insure an easy companionship for the remainder of their journey. In time to come, Marius was to depend very much on the preferences, the personal judgments, of the comrade who now laid his hand so brotherly on his shoulder" (Pater, *Marius*, I, p. 168).

However, typical Uranian posturing involves an aesthetic proximity to the object of desire without that voyeuristic distance ever being transgressed, as is illustrated in *Peter Pan*, in *The Plays of J. M. Barrie* (London: Hodder and Stoughton, 1936), pp. 1-90 (pp. 29-30):

> *Wendy*: Peter!
> (*She leaps out of bed to put her arms round him, but he draws back; he does not know why, but he knows he must draw back*)
> *Peter*: You mustn't touch me.
> *Wendy*: Why?
> *Peter*: No one must ever touch me.
> *Wendy*: Why?
> *Peter*: I don't know.
> (*He is never touched by any one in the play*)

23 As early as his "Diaphaneitè" essay, presented before the Old Mortality Society in Oxford in July 1864, Pater cautioned against squandering opportunities, insisting that "to most of us only one chance is given in the life of the spirit and the intellect, and circumstances prevent our dexterously seizing that one chance"—in *Miscellaneous Studies: A Series of Essays*, 1st edn (London: Macmillan, 1895), pp. 215-222 (p. 220).

24 See Introduction. "In my reading of Greek poetry and philosophy I was principally busy to find a confirmation of my private point of view. [....] It was a paganism softened, orientalized, I dare say, to bring it into accord with what I desired; nevertheless, what appealed to me was to be found in the literature of Greece, and not elsewhere" (Reid, *Apostate*, p. 206). From the 2nd edition (1877) forward, *The Renaissance* has included a consideration of *Li Amitiez de Ami et Amile*, a thirteenth-century French romance, the addition of which allows Pater to connect "medieval, Christian culture with the tradition of homosexual friendship in Greek culture"—Richard Dellamora, "An Essay in Sexual Liberation, Victorian Style: Walter Pater's 'Two Early French Stories'," in *Literary Visions of Homosexuality*, ed. by Stuart Kellogg (New York: Haworth, 1983), pp. 139-50 (p. 143). According to Pater, Amis and Amile had "a friendship pure and generous, pushed to a sort of passionate exaltation, and more than faithful unto death. Such comradeship, though instances of it are to be found everywhere, is still especially a classical motive" (*Renaissance* 1893, p. 7). "[Emerald] finds the Greek or the Latin model of their antique

friendship or tries to find it, in the books they read together. None fits exactly"—Pater, "Emerald Uthwart," p. 185.

25   Although more famously elaborated in his poem *Epipsychidion*, Percy Bysshe Shelley encapsulates this concept in his essay "On Love": "A soul within our soul that describes a circle around its proper Paradise which pain and sorrow and evil dare not overleap"—"On Love," in *Shelley's Poetry and Prose*, ed. by Donald H. Reiman and Sharon B. Powers (London: Norton, 1977), pp. 473-74.

26   As a questioning invocation, this passage from Shelley's "Hymn to Intellectual Beauty," lines 13-15 (in Reiman and Powers, ed., *Shelley's Poetry and Prose*, pp. 93-95), is particularly important to consider, for it sets the tone and serves to forecast much that will happen in *The Garden God*, especially given the entire stanza from which it comes:

> Spirit of BEAUTY, that dost consecrate
>   With thine own hues all thou dost shine upon
>   Of human thought or form,—where art thou gone?
> Why dost thou pass away and leave our state,
> This dim vast vale of tears, vacant and desolate?
>   Ask why the sunlight not forever
>   Weaves rainbows o'er yon mountain river,
> Why aught should fail and fade that once is shewn,
>   Why fear and dream and death and birth
>   Cast on the daylight of this earth
>   Such gloom,—why man has such a scope
> For love and hate, despondency and hope?

27   This is a common claim in any form of Uranian apologia:

> Just there, then, is the secret of Plato's intimate concern with, his power over, the sensible world, the apprehensions of the sensuous faculty: he is a lover, a great lover, somewhat after the manner of Dante.

> Few modern writers, when they speak with admiration or contempt of Platonic love, reflect that in its origin this phrase denoted an absorbing passion for young men.

> The "Love that dare not speak its name" in this century is such a great affection of an elder for a younger man as there was between David and Jonathan, such as Plato made the very basis of his philosophy, and such as you find in the sonnets of Michaelangelo and Shakespeare. It is that deep, spiritual affection that is as pure as it is perfect.

Quoted respectively: Walter Pater, *Plato and Platonism*, p. 135; J. A. Symonds, *Greek Ethics*, p. 54; from Wilde's apologia during the first of

his two trials for "gross indecency," 1895—as quoted in Ellmann, *Wilde*,
p. 463.

28   Percy Bysshe Shelley, "The Indian Girl's Song" [also known as "The
Indian Serenade"], lines 1-8 (in Reiman and Powers, ed., *Shelley's Poetry
and Prose*, pp. 369-71).

29   In March 1882, the *Journal of Education* (152.49), pp. 85-86, published a
lengthy letter, signed "Olim Etonensis," arguing that educators should
"let well alone" and not interfere in the immoral practices of the boys
in their charge, since these practices have no lingering repercussions—
see d'Arch Smith, p. 2. The poet Rupert Brooke (1887-1915), whom
Reid knew from Cambridge, was reported to have observed, while
temporarily a housemaster at Rugby: "What is the whole duty of a
housemaster? To prepare boys for Confirmation, and turn a blind
eye on sodomy"—as quoted in John Knowler, *Trust an Englishman*
(Harmondsworth, Middlesex, UK: Penguin, 1972), pp. 121-22. See also
Vern and Bonnie Bullough, "Homosexuality in Nineteenth Century
English Public Schools," in *Homosexuality in International Perspective*, ed.
by Joseph Harry and Man Singh Das (New Delhi, India: Vikas, 1980), pp.
123-31; John Chandos, *Boys Together: English Public Schools, 1800-1864* (New
Haven, CT: Yale University Press, 1984); Alisdare Hickson, *The Poisoned
Bowl: Sex, Repression and the Public School System* (London: Constable,
1995).

30   Reid seems to be echoing, intentionally, one of the most masterfully
handled erotic moments in English literature, the bedroom seduction
scene in chapter XVII of Henry James's *The Turn of the Screw*:

> "Then you weren't asleep?" [asks the governess.]
> "Not much! I lie awake and think."
> I had put my candle, designedly, a short way off, and then, as he held out
> his friendly old hand to me, had sat down on the edge of his bed. "What is it,"
> I asked, "that you think of?"
> "What in the world, my dear, but *you*?"

—*The Turn of the Screw* [New York edn], in *Complete Stories, 1892-1898*
(New York: Library of America, 1996), pp. 635-740 (p. 709).

31   This recalls Walter Pater's consideration of the neutral angels. In a
passing comment on Matteo Palmieri's *La Città di Vita* (1464), Pater
demarcates a position outside of society for himself and his defiant
Uranian followers by lending symbolic virtue to the human "incarnation
of those angels who, in the revolt of Lucifer, were neither for Jehovah
nor for His enemies" ("Sandro Botticelli," *Renaissance* 1893, p. 42), those
scurrilous spirits whom Dante relegates to the Vestibule of Hell as
"unworthy alike of heaven and hell, [...] [occupying instead] that middle

world in which men take no side in great conflicts, and decide no great causes, and make great refusals" (p. 43).

32 Such nocturnal escapes are so common in Reid's works that they are almost an expectation. As he playfully notes in an issue of *Kenneth's Magazine* (see Taylor, *Green*, pp. 88-90):

> I sing about wonderful boys,
> Who wander about at night,
> With surprising absence of noise,
> And no single smyton of fright,
> If you ask them in accents faint
> Why their manner's so very quaint,
> They will say "it's the natural taint,
> You're wrong if you think it ain't."

33 This is an ancient musical instrument, also known as the "syrinx," based on the principle of the stopped pipe, consisting usually of ten or more pipes of gradually increasing length. "Pan, who loved the rocks and woods, was associated in my mind with music, the music of leaves and running water and his own pipes" (Reid, *Apostate*, p. 211).

34 In "The Portrait of Mr. W. H.," in *Complete Works*, pp. 302-50 (pp. 319-20), Oscar Wilde's narrator asserts:

> So well had Shakespeare drawn [Willie Hughes], with his golden hair, his tender flower-like grace, his dreamy deep-sunken eyes, his delicate mobile limbs, and his white lily hands. His very name fascinated me. Willie Hughes! Willie Hughes! How musically it sounded! Yes; who else but he could have been the master-mistress of Shakespeare's passion, the lord of his love to whom he was bound in vassalage, the delicate minion of pleasure, the rose of the whole world, the herald of the spring decked in the proud livery of youth, the lovely boy whom it was sweet music to hear, and whose beauty was the very raiment of Shakespeare's heart [...]

The following is from whence Reid's catalogue of Shakespearean epithets derives: *"lord of his love"* (*Sonnets*, XXVI, line 1; "Lord of my love"), *"herald of the spring"* (I, line 10; "herald to the gaudy spring"), *"lovely boy"* (CXXVI, line 1), *"rose of beauty"* (I, line 2; "beauty's rose"), *"music to hear"* (VIII, line 1), *"For all that beauty [. . .]"* (XXII, lines 5-6); *"Shall I compare thee [. . .]"* (XVIII, lines 1-5). Although the majority of these derive verbatim from Shakespeare's *Sonnets*, several are instead verbatim from the passage above by Wilde, suggesting that this may have been the mediated source. See "Introduction," p. xxii, for Reid's ancestral connection to one of the candidates for the elusive "Mr. W. H."

35 These two poems are transformed into Uranian texts through Graham's subsequent comment about "altering the gender." Excerpts from these poems appear as "Appendix Three" and "Four," with "The Stream's Secret" taken from Dante Gabriel Rossetti, *Poems, A New Edition* (London: Ellis & White, 1881), pp. 103-14; "Love's Nocturn," from ibid., pp. 95-102. This re-gendering represents a curious cultural twist, since it has often been the case that homoerotic and pederastic writing has, out of necessity, done the opposite. In essence, Reid is decadently suggesting the possibility of an endless collection of same-sex writing, made by intrusively (re)claiming traditional, "heterosexual" verse as its own.

"Everything connected with what appeared to me to be my more real life I had to keep hidden. For there is nobody, perhaps, quite so conventional, in his own queer way, as the average schoolboy. I knew [. . .] it would never do to say there was a poet called Rossetti who had written lovely things—*The Blessed Damozel, The Stream's Secret, My Sister's Sleep*" (Reid, *Apostate*, pp. 195-96).

36 These are Grecian "spirits of water and land." *Hamadryads* are nymphs bonded to specific trees, trees whose fates are linked to their own. *Oreads* are nymphs presiding over mountains, valleys, and ravines, the most famous of which is probably Echo. *Naiads* are nymphs presiding over fountains, springs, marshes, rivers, and lakes. "*Hyades* [are] those first leaping mænads, who, as the springs become rain-clouds, go up to heaven among the stars, and descend again, as dew or shower, upon it; so that the religion of Dionysus connects itself, not with tree-worship only, but also with ancient water-worship, the worship of the *spiritual forms* of springs and streams"—Walter Pater, "A Study of Dionysus," in *Greek Studies*, pp. 1-48 (pp. 20-21).

37 Pater, "Dionysus," *Greek Studies*, pp. 15-16:

Of the whole story of Dionysus, it was the episode of his marriage with Ariadne about which ancient art concerned itself oftenest, and with most effect. [....] And as a story of romantic love, fullest perhaps of all the motives of classic legend of the pride of life, it survived with undiminished interest to a later world. [....] Hardly less humanised is the Theban legend of Dionysus, the legend of his birth from Semele, which, out of the entire body of tradition concerning him, was accepted as central by the Athenian imagination.

38 See note 41, "the cool shallow stream up which Socrates and Phaedrus had walked [...]"

39 Benjamin Jowett, trans., *Phaedo*, in *The Dialogues of Plato translated into English with Analyses and Introductions by B. Jowett, M.A. in Five Volumes,*

3rd edn, rev. and corrected (London: Oxford University Press, 1892), II, pp. 157-266 (p. 206).

40 Matthew 5:8 (KJV). This seems particularly innocent, a blending of the Christian and the Platonic that Reid has sometimes been credited with attempting to actualise, as with "the biblical story of Jonathan and David," a story that "reinforces the Greek ideal of friendship that Reid adapted to modern time"—Mary Bryan, *Forrest Reid* (Boston: G. K. Hall, 1976), p. 61. However, this particular verse involving "the pure in heart" also contained, for the Uranians, an imbedded pederastic suggestiveness, with the word "pure" playfully constituting *puer* (Latin for "boy").

41 Benjamin Jowett, trans., *Phaedrus*, in *The Dialogues of Plato translated into English with Analyses and Introductions by B. Jowett, M.A. in Five Volumes*, 3rd edn, rev. and corrected (London: Oxford University Press, 1892), I, pp. 391-489 (pp. 433-35).

42 Jowett, trans., *Phaedrus*, p. 489:

> *Socrates*: Beloved Pan, and all ye other gods who haunt this place, give me beauty in the inward soul; and may the outward and inward man be at one. May I reckon the wise to be the wealthy, and may I have such a quantity of gold as a temperate man and he only can bear and carry.— Anything more? The prayer, I think, is enough for me.

43 By considering Plato's *Phaedrus* directly before considering a set of Dutch genre paintings, Reid seems to have in mind the following passage (*Marius*, I, p. 32), where we are told that Pater's Marius the Epicurean is equally driven by

> the capacity of the eye, inasmuch as in the eye would lie for him the determining influence of life: he was of the number of those who, in the words of a poet who came long after, must be "made perfect by the love of visible beauty." The discourse was conceived from the point of view of a theory Marius found afterwards in Plato's *Phaedrus*, which supposes men's spirits susceptible to certain influences, diffused, after the manner of streams or currents, by fair things or persons visibly present—green fields, for instance, or children's faces—into the air around them, acting, in the case of some peculiar natures, like potent material essences, and conforming the seer to themselves as with some cunning physical necessity.

44 Pieter de Hooch (1629-84) was a Dutch genre painter whose works exhibit themes and stylistic elements similar to those of his contemporary Jan Vermeer. Gerard ter Borch (or Terburg) (1617-81) was a Dutch genre painter. Adrian van de Velde (1636-72) was a Dutch animal and landscape painter. Gerard Dou (1613-75), a pupil of Rembrandt van Rijn, was a Dutch artist given to fine detail.

45 More often than not, the Uranians advocated "The New Chivalry"; hence, they were against democratic institutions, recognising that aristocracy was more compatible, in many ways, with the hierarchical pederasty they lauded. In *The Desire and Pursuit of the Whole*, ed. by Andrew Eburne (New York: Braziller, 1994 [1934]), p. 238, Frederick Rolfe's protagonist Nicholas Crabbe is contemplating his as-yet-unwritten treatise titled *Towards Aristocracy*, an attack against and a corrective to Edward Carpenter's egalitarian *Towards Democracy*.

46 This allusion to Samuel Taylor Coleridge's "The Rime of the Ancient Mariner," in *Lyrical Ballads* (1798), is the first of a series of allusions having to do with memory.

47 "Calypso the lustrous goddess tried to hold me back, deep in her arching caverns, craving me for a husband. So did Circe, holding me just as warmly in her halls, the bewitching queen of Aeaea keen to have me too"—Homer, *Odyssey*, trans. by Fagles, p. 212 (IX, lines 33-36). "Odysseus's lack of geographical orientation when he arrives on Circe's island foreshadows his loss of existential direction. For the first and last time, his mind, 'which cannot be enchanted,' forgets. Circe urges Odysseus and his comrades to recover their spirits by forgetting their wanderings"—Silvia Montiglio, *Wandering in Ancient Greek Culture* (Chicago: University of Chicago Press, 2005), p. 58.

48 "Any crewman who ate the lotus [. . .] only wish[ed] to linger there with the Lotus-eaters, gazing on lotus, all memory of the journey home dissolved forever"—Homer, *Odyssey*, trans. by Fagles, p. 214 (IX, lines 106-10). Although the most famous treatment of this theme during the nineteenth century was that of Alfred, Lord Tennyson, it was handled by a multitude of other poets and artists. See Christina Rossetti, "The Lotus-Eaters: Ulysses to Penelope," lines 1-26, in *Poetical Works*, p. 111.

49 In Homer's *Odyssey*, Nausicaa, a Phaeacian princess, is inspired by Athena, in a dream, to do the laundry herself, during which she discovers the shipwrecked Odysseus on the shore. Through her and Athena's interventions, Odysseus is able to return home, with Odysseus promising to remember her: "Nausicaa, daughter of generous King Alcinous, may Zeus the Thunderer, Hera's husband, grant it so—that I travel home and see the dawn of my return. Even at home I'll pray to you as a deathless goddess all my days to come. You saved my life, dear girl"—Homer, *Odyssey*, trans. by Fagles, p. 206 (VIII, lines 522-26).

50 As the last consideration of remembrance, this allusion to the story of Narcissus inserts a pederastic dynamic into the sequence. Although expurgated from later versions of the tale, in the original myth the fate of Narcissus is determined by his rejection of even pederastic love:

Narcissus was sixteen now, and his beauty blazed full force. [....] His neighbor, Ameinias, loved him more than all the others [....] The boy, of course, paid him scant notice. Finally, out of his wits with longing, Ameinias waylaid Narcissus. He bared his heart, begged him to be his beloved. Narcissus held his tongue. A sharpened dagger, sent with a slave, was his answer. Ameinias caught on. He stood on Narcissus' doorstep, lifted his hands to the skies, called down the wrath of the gods upon the one who spurned him: "Let him, too, be consumed by love ... and let him be denied the one he craves!" Then he turned the dagger on himself.

—Andrew Calimach, *Lovers' Legends: The Gay Greek Myths* (New Rochelle, NY: Haiduk Press, 2002), pp. 95-96. See also Steven Bruhm, "Reforming Byron's Narcissism," in *Lessons of Romanticism: A Critical Companion*, ed. by Thomas Pfau and Robert F. Gleckner (Durham, NC: Duke University Press, 1998), pp. 429-47 (p. 431).

51 See Oscar Wilde, "The Young King," in *The Complete Works of Oscar Wilde*, 3rd edn (Glasgow: Harper Collins, 1994), pp. 213-22 (p. 213). This comparison of the belovèd to some form of Greco-Roman deity is a Uranian stereotype. Considering Flavian to be his "epitome of the whole pagan world" and "his own Cyrenaic philosophy [...] in an image or person" (I, pp. 53; 234), Pater's Marius thought him "like a carved figure in motion [...] but with that indescribable gleam upon it which the words of Homer actually suggested, as perceptible on the visible forms of the gods" (I, p. 50).

However, the phrase "far nicer than the statue" suggests that Graham is referring to a specific sculpture. Perhaps he is referring to the famous *Barberini Faun*, a marble sculpture discovered in the Mausoleum of Hadrian, Rome, and now in the Staatliche Antiksammlungen und Glyptotech, Munich, Germany. This Roman copy (ca. 230-200 BCE) of a Greek original was heavily restored by Gian Lorenzo Bernini in the 17th century. Perhaps Graham is referring to the "Faun of Praxiteles," invented by Nathaniel Hawthorne for his romance *The Marble Faun* (1860) but based on the *Statue of a Resting Satyr*, a marble in the Musei Capitolini, Rome, that is commonly considered a copy of a lost sculpture by Praxiteles (4th century BCE).

52 This sculpture—dating to around 300 BCE and in the tradition of Lysipp, a Greek sculptor—is in the Staatliche Museen zu Berlin. Walter Pater, "The Age of Athletic Prizemen," in *Greek Studies*: "The Adorante of Berlin, Winckelmann's antique favourite, who with uplifted face and hands seems to be indeed in prayer, looks immaculate enough to be interceding for others" (p. 315).

53 Reid probably had in mind J. A. Symonds's essay "In the Key of Blue," from *In the Key of Blue and Other Prose Essays* (London: Elkin Mathews,

1918 [1893]), pp. 1-16: "It struck me that it would be amusing to try the resources of our language in a series of studies of what might be termed 'blues and blouses.' For this purpose I resolved to take a single figure—a *facchino* [porter] with whom I have been long acquainted—and to pose him in a variety of lights with a variety of hues in combination" (pp. 4-5).

54   This *Bacchus*, in the Musée du Louvre, Paris, is an oil painting that was transferred from its original panel to canvas. It is now dated 1510-15 and attributed to the workshop of Leonardo da Vinci (1452-1519). See Walter Pater, "Leonardo da Vinci," in *The Renaissance*, pp. 77-101, especially pp. 93-94.

55   This is the *genius loci*, or "guardian deity of the place." In *Nature and the Idea of a Man-Made World: An Investigation into the Evolutionary Roots of Form and Order in the Built Environment* (Cambridge, MA: MIT Press, 1995), p. 75, Norman Crowe considers the Roman belief in *genius loci*:

> These spirits, or *genius loci*, reflected the uniqueness of a place, distinguishing one place from other places with which it might be confused. They inhabited all places of significance. A spirit would own a place, look after it, and imbue it with sense and meaning. [....] The *genius loci*'s consummate duty was to provide a protective presence, thereby animating what would otherwise be an inert, impersonal incident in the landscape, the villa, or the city.

56   See also Reid, *Garden God*, p. 70. This is partially a reference to Acts 17:22-29, where Paul, in Athens, encounters a temple dedicated to *Agnostos Theos*, or "the Unknown God." See also Alfred Austin, "Profane Love Speaks," in *Sacred and Profane Love and Other Poems* (London: Macmillan, 1908), lines 291-98; Edward Carpenter, "To the Unknown God," in *Sketches from Life in Town and Country* (London: George Allen, [1908]); Forrest Reid, "Pan's Pupil" ("Appendix One," pp. 93-96).

57   Elizabeth Barrett Browning, "The Dead Pan," lines 1-7, in *The Complete Poetical Works of Elizabeth Barrett Browning* (London: Houghton, Mifflin, 1900), pp. 408-11:

> Gods of Hellas, gods of Hellas,
> Can ye listen in your silence?
> Can your mystic voices tell us
> Where ye hide? In floating islands,
> With a wind that evermore
> Keeps you out of sight of shore?
> Pan, Pan is dead.

58   In *Love Between Men in English Literature* (New York: St. Martin's, 1996), Paul Hammond acknowledges this "trope," however authentic: "Much

of the pederastic writing of the nineteenth century delights in imagining boys wounded or dead" (p. 142). See Kincaid, *Child-Loving*, p. 226. Occasionally, this trope became rather macabre, as in Reid's note for a planned, but never written, story: "Story of a man revisiting a school, now abandoned, finds in a cupboard the skeleton of a boy who must have been there in his time ... suddenly aware of the shade of one of the masters watching him—feels the only thing to be done is to bury the skeleton as quietly as possible" (as quoted in Taylor, *Green*, p. 176).

The earlier allusion to Hippolytus (on p. 60) serves to foreshadow both Harold's demise and the method by which it is brought about. In mythology, Hippolytus (Greek for "loose horse"), a son of Theseus and either Antiope or Hippolyte, is later associated with the Roman god of the forest, Virbius. Alfred Bates (ed.), *The Drama: Its History, Literature and Influence on Civilization*, 20 vols (London: Historical Publishing, 1906 [1903]), I, p. 70:

> Of the extant plays of Euripides, the Hippolytus, which took the first prize at its reproduction in 428 B.C., deserves the highest place. In the prologue, Aphrodite declares herself resolved to punish the chaste Hippolytus, son of Theseus, who disdains her and pays his worship to Artemis. With this design she has put into the heart of Phaedra, the wife of Theseus, a love for her stepson. This Theseus will learn, and then will destroy his son by one of three fatal wishes which Poseidon has promised to fulfill. This will involve the ruin of Phaedra too, but for that there is no help, the goddess caring first for her honor and herself. Presently Hippolytus enters; he lauds his lady Artemis and consecrates to her a garland. An attendant suggests that he should in like manner honor Aphrodite, whose statue also stands at the entrance to the palace. Hippolytus, deaf to advice, persists in ignoring the goddess, and therein lies his offense.

59   This passage, also quoted in *The Picture of Dorian Gray*, is from the famous balcony scene in Shakespeare's *Romeo and Juliet*, Act II, scene 2, lines 112-29.

60   Graham's argument for the immortality of the soul recalls Pater's "Conclusion" to *The Renaissance* (p. 189):

> To burn always with this hard, gem-like flame, to maintain this ecstasy, is success in life. In a sense it might even be said that our failure is to form habits: for, after all, habit is relative to a stereotyped world, and meantime it is only the roughness of the eye that makes any two persons, things, situations, seem alike. While all melts under our feet, we may well grasp at any exquisite passion, or any contribution to knowledge that seems by a lifted horizon to set the spirit free for a moment, or any stirring of the senses, strange dyes, strange colours, and curious odours, or work of the artist's hands, or the face of one's friend.

61   This is the last stanza of Dante Gabriel Rossetti's "The Stream's Secret."
      See "Appendix Three", pp. 98-99.
62   John 13:33-34 and 15:12-13 (KJV).
63   The very end of this short novel recalls Alfred, Lord Tennyson's poem
      "Mariana." See Reid, *Apostate*, p. 185; *Young Tom*, pp. 60-61.

— APPENDIX ONE —

Pan's Pupil[1]

Forrest Reid

'Rich in the simple worship of a day' —John Keats

The boy passed out into the garden, where for a few minutes he wandered among the flowers, shaking the dew from the heavy crimson roses, and burying his face among their cool, drenched leaves. The sunlight lay on the grass all around him, every living thing was glad and happy, and innumerable birds were singing to the summer god. They sang of the joy of life and of love, of the charm of nests among green leaves, and of the impossibility of the warm weather's ever coming to an end. The boy's own heart began to be strangely uplifted, and he ran across the lawn and down a wooded slope leading to the river bank. There, in the cool fresh grass powdered with daisies, he seated himself, hugging his chin against his knees, and gazing down through the deep, clear, sunlit water. On the opposite bank grew a willow. It drooped so low that the tips of its branches rested upon the surface of the river, and when the wind blew among them the long slender leaves seemed to caress the water and to whisper to it as it passed. The boy rolled over and over in the long cool grass, the earth-smell in his nostrils, the earth-murmur in his ears.

From time to time a faint rustle passed through the tree-tops, like the whisper of a spirit, but down where the boy lay there was only shelter and summer heat. He felt supremely lazy and happy, and presently, taking a shepherd's pipe from his pocket, he began to blow into it very softly and dreamily—so softly, so dreamily, that a little blackbird with a yellow bill, who had been hopping about among the green boughs overhead, stood still for a moment, and peeped down to see what was the matter. And from time to time

---

[1] Originally published in *Ulad: A Literary and Critical Magazine*, 1.3 (May 1905), pp. 17-19.

the boy smiled and the notes he played died into silence, as he built his castles in the air and watched them climb like towers toward the sky and crumble into dust.

He sat with his back against the gray, gnarled trunk of a tree, his straw hat pushed back from his forehead, the sunlight asleep in his soft gold hair; and whether it was suggested by his piping, or whether it was merely the beauty of the summer morning that made him think of it, he could never afterwards tell, but the old pagan world seemed in some unaccountable way to have drawn very close to him, and he could half believe that through the leafy shadows of the trees he saw the dim paleness of a god, could half believe that he heard a low sound of a voice in the sleepy noon-tide hum, and in the faint noise of falling water coming from the weir. And presently from the deep slumbrous quiet there slid into the boy's soul a gentle drowsiness, as a light summer shower sinks down into the soil.

He lay very still, gazing up through the golden quivering heat at the sky, so soft, so pure, so far-off, so untroubled by mortal joys and sorrows, and he began to wonder vaguely just where in all that immensity was the country of the gods. His brown slender hands rested motionless on either side on the grass; and over all the landscape there lay the heavy, aching sunlight.

Suddenly he was awakened from his reverie by the sound of the breaking of a branch, and by a voice that seemed to pass above his head. 'Follow; follow,' it seemed to cry; 'oh, follow quickly.' He started up, and thought he saw a dim white form disappearing among the trees; and then the voice sounded again, but this time from the very heart of the wood—'Follow, follow!'

'Little piper, do you know into whose kingdom you have strayed?' He who spoke was a man, no longer young, dark like some statue of dark bronze, and naked. His thick shaggy hair curled over his low forehead, his features were ill-formed, his ears pointed, but his eyes were gentle.

The boy clasped his hands about his knees. He shook his head. 'I do not know,' he made answer, 'but I think you must be Pan.'

'Did you not call me to you? Do not be afraid. I will not harm you. You are a human boy, and must live out your destiny. I will not keep you. Someday, however, when the world seems very hard and cold, you will perhaps seek again the door to my fairyland, and if you find it then and enter, it will be to stay for ever and ever. You are a child, and I am very old, yet I will be here when you return.'

'But are you not a god, and can the gods grow old?'

Pan shook his head. 'I was a god in Sicily when you were a shepherd boy; and they gave me a grotto on the side of the Acropolis hill at Athens. But among the Olympians I have no place. Eternal youth is not mine, as you may easily see,' he added, with a strange, half-smiling tenderness. 'Already I feel the creeping snows of old age in my blood; and though your love to-day has warmed my heart a little, as the winter is warmed by the sun, yet am I still the winter, and when you have left me night will follow quickly.'

As he spoke, the boy looked into his eyes, and it was as if already he gazed into the darkness of that eternal night. And slowly, slowly, the river and the fields and the trees and the sky itself seemed to shrink together, and to fade away like smoke, while a cold deathly wind from some sunken well of space older than the world blew past his cheek. He shut his eyes and clenched his hands tightly; and his soul seemed to be drawn out from his body, and in a few minutes to live through endless ages. But gradually, through the darkness, he saw the breaking of a dawn—a light reaching back—back into the morning of the world. He saw a countryside rich with green grass and slender flowers. He saw faint sleepy poppies, and bending fields of corn. He saw the first beauty of the earth, of silver streams, and golden woods, and violet valleys, and tree-shaded water springs. He saw, in forest glades, fauns and nymphs dancing under the red harvest-moon, and beside haunted pools in whose still water the over-world was mirrored. And he knew that from all these things he had drawn the strength of his life, and he dropped upon his knees and cried: 'O Pan, I am your child for evermore, and none save Death shall take me from you.'

'And Death is far away.' The words dropped from the god's lips like an echo from the golden house of sleep; and for a moment his brown, withered hand rested on the boy's hair. 'Yet death, for those who are a little tired, is not unlovely; and it is so long since the morning. . . . a shadow creeping across a river—that river whose dark water is the dreaming of the world—and then the night.'

The boy closed his eyes. For just a moment Pan's voice had seemed to send the hush of twilight into his soul; but the sunshine conquered again, and the simple instinct of youth. 'Why should you not live for ever?' he asked. 'Have you not heard of a gentle god who came into the world to put an end to suffering and sorrow—one who, like you, wandered in the fields and valleys, and whose roof was the open sky? He had the secret of a certain water that bestowed everlasting life, and he gave of this water unto all who asked of it.'

'I have heard of him,' Pan answered slowly, doubtfully. 'For a little, I think, he wandered in the world; and then he was seen no more. Like Dionysus he came out of the East, and was pale with the burden of his dreams. But of the water of youth I know nothing. Nay, was not he of whom you speak slain by his own disciples?—a philosopher rather than a god, a poet, a dreamer, a lover of flowers and gardens and of a life untroubled by riches and the cares of the world. But I forget. Only I know that in the past his priests tore down my altars. They tore down my altars, and yet I am to-day the spirit of the earth, and I am worshipped in the beauty of each passing hour.'

The god's voice died slowly away, and his last words seemed to come from a distance, and to melt in the rustling of the trees. And Pan himself was fading—fading back into a green dimness that was soon but the deep shadow of the wood. Had there ever been anything there but that shadow? Had his fancy played him a trick? Had he been asleep, and was it all only a dream? Presently the boy rose to his feet and walked slowly homeward. But in his heart the leaves were whispering still, and deep down in his soul he knew that one day he must return.

— APPENDIX TWO —

SPINARIO

The Thorn-Puller

Hellenistic Greek
Bronze, ca. 1st century BCE
Sala dei Trionfi
Museo del Palazzo dei Conservatori, Rome

— APPENDIX THREE —

From "THE STREAM'S SECRET"

Dante Gabriel Rossetti[1]

> What thing unto mine ear
> Wouldst thou convey,—what secret thing,
> O wandering water ever whispering?
> Surely thy speech shall be of him.
> Thou water, O thou whispering wanderer,
> What message dost thou bring?
>
> Say, hath not Love leaned low
> This hour beside thy far well-head,
> And there through jealous hollowed fingers said
> The thing that most I long to know,—
> Murmuring with curls all dabbled in thy flow
> And washed lips rosy red?
>
> He told it to thee there
> Where thy voice hath a louder tone;
> But where it welters to this little moan
> His will decrees that I should hear.
> Now speak: for with the silence is no fear,
> And I am all alone.
>
> Shall Time not still endow
> One hour with life, and I and he
> Slake in one kiss the thirst of memory?
> Say, stream; lest Love should disavow
> Thy service, and the bird upon the bough
> Sing first to tell it me.

. . . .

---

[1] The text has been altered in accordance with Graham's practice of 'altering the gender' (*Garden God*, p. 40).

But he is far away
   Now; nor the hours of night grown hoar
Bring yet to me, long gazing from the door,
   The wind-stirred robe of roseate grey
And rose-crown of the hour that leads the day
      When we shall meet once more.

   Dark as thy blinded wave
When brimming midnight floods the glen,—
Bright as the laughter of thy runnels when
   The dawn yields all the light they crave;
Even so these hours to wound and that to save
      Are brothers in Love's ken.

   Oh sweet his bending grace
Then when I kneel beside his feet;
And sweet his eyes' o'erhanging heaven; and sweet
   The gathering folds of his embrace;
And his fall'n hair at last shed round my face
      When breaths and tears shall meet.

   Beneath his sheltering hair,
In the warm silence near his breast,
Our kisses and our sobs shall sink to rest;
   As in some still trance made aware
That day and night have wrought to fulness there
      And Love has built our nest.

. . . .

   O water whispering
Still through the dark into mine ears,—
As with mine eyes, is it not now with his?—
   Mine eyes that add to thy cold spring,
Wan water, wandering water weltering,
      This hidden tide of tears.

— APPENDIX FOUR —

From "Love's Nocturn"

Dante Gabriel Rossetti[1]

Vaporous, unaccountable,
  Dreamland lies forlorn of light,
Hollow like a breathing shell.
    Ah! that from all dreams I might
    Choose one dream and guide its flight!
       I know well
    What his sleep should tell to-night.

. . . .

Reft of him, my dreams are all
  Clammy trance that fears the sky:
Changing footpaths shift and fall;
    From polluted coverts nigh,
    Miserable phantoms sigh;
       Quakes the pall,
    And the funeral goes by.

Master, is it soothly said
  That, as echoes of man's speech
Far in secret clefts are made,
    So do all men's bodies reach
    Shadows o'er thy sunken beach,—
       Shape or shade
    In those halls pourtrayed of each?

Ah! might I, by thy good grace
  Groping in the windy stair,
(Darkness and the breath of space
    Like loud waters everywhere,)
    Meeting mine own image there
       Face to face,
    Send it from that place to him!

---

[1] The text has been altered in accordance with Graham's practice of 'altering the gender' (*Garden God*, p. 40).

Nay, not I; but oh! do thou,
    Master, from thy shadowkind
Call my body's phantom now:
    Bid it bear its face declin'd
    Till its flight his slumbers find,
                And his brow
    Feel its presence bow like wind.

. . . .

Not the prayers which with all leave
    The world's fluent woes prefer,—
Not the praise the world doth give,
    Dulcet fulsome whisperer;—
    Let it yield my love to him,
                And achieve
    Strength that shall not grieve or err.

Wheresoe'er my dreams befall,
    Both at night-watch, (let it say,)
And where round the sundial
    The reluctant hours of day,
    Heartless, hopeless of their way,
                Rest and call;—
    There his glance doth fall and stay.

Suddenly his face is there:
    So do mounting vapours wreathe
Subtle-scented transports where
    The black firwood sets its teeth.
    Part the boughs and look beneath,—
                Lilies share
    Secret waters there, and breathe.

. . . .

Yet, ah me! if at his head
    There another phantom lean
Murmuring o'er the fragrant bed,—
    Ah! and if my spirit's king
    Smile those alien prayers between,—
                Ah! poor shade!
    Shall it strive, or fade unseen?

How should love's own messenger
   Strive with love and be love's foe?
Master, nay! If thus, in him,
   Sleep a wedded heart should show,—
   Silent let mine image go,
         Its old share
   Of thy spell-bound air to know.

. . . .

Yea, to Love himself is pour'd
   This frail song of hope and fear.
Thou art Love, of one accord
   With kind Sleep to bring him near,
   Still-eyed, deep-eyed, ah, how dear!
        Master, Lord,
   In his name implor'd, O hear!

9 781934 555040